MW01147971

PURRFECT OBSESSION

THE MYSTERIES OF MAX 10

NIC SAINT

PUSS IN PRINT PUBLICATIONS

PURRFECT OBSESSION

The Mysteries of Max 10

Copyright © 2019 by Nic Saint

All rights reserved. No part of this book may be reproduced in any form by any electronic or mechanical means including photocopying, recording, or information storage and retrieval without permission in writing from the author.

This is a work of fiction. Names, characters, places, brands, media, and incidents are either the product of the author's imagination or are used fictitiously. The author acknowledges the trademarked status and trademark owners of various products referenced in this work of fiction, which have been used without permission. The publication/use of these trademarks is not authorized, associated with, or sponsored by the trademark owners.

Edited by Chereese Graves

www.nicsaint.com

Give feedback on the book at: info@nicsaint.com

facebook.com/nicsaintauthor
@nicsaintauthor

First Edition

Printed in the U.S.A

I was lying on my back in the backyard, languidly gazing up at the clouds slowly drifting past my field of vision. My paws were dangling wherever they might, my tail was drooping, and it wasn't too much to say that all was well in this best of all worlds.

Some would have called it the calm before the storm, but they would be cynics. This wasn't the calm before the storm. This was the calm after the storm, as there had been rain overnight, and the grass was still soggy and drops clung to Odelia's roses' petals.

Next to me, my best friend and co-feline Dooley lay in the same position, also idly gazing up at the sky. There was apprehension in his gaze, though, his usual response to looking at that big slice of heaven up above. His eternal fear is that a piece of this heaven might one day come crashing down on us. And no matter how many times I've assured him that this is simply impossible, there's no way to dissuade him from these erroneous ideas.

"I don't know, Max," he said now, shaking his head.

"What don't you know?" I murmured, my eyes drifting closed. There's only so much to look at when you're gazing at the sky. It's blue and all looks pretty much the same to me.

"I don't know about this lying around, doing absolutely nothing."

"It's what us cats do best," I said. "We lie around doing nothing."

"But it just feels... wrong, you know."

"No, I don't know. What are you talking about?"

"This ... " He gestured at the sky. "And this..." he added, indicating the smooth lawn that was our favorite hangout spot on a sunny day like this—especially after a nice storm.

"I don't get it, Dooley," I said lazily. "Please elaborate."

"I just don't understand how you can lie around while there's so much to be done."

"Nothing needs to be done," I said, my eyes now having closed completely, my head slumping to the side. I felt a power nap coming on, and nothing Dooley said was going to prevent me from enjoying it tremendously.

"There's probably murder cases to be solved."

"Not a single one."

"Or-or missing humans to be found?"

"Nobody's gone missing as far as I know."

"Dangerous diseases to be fought? Pests to be eradicated? Threats to be thwarted? Max! We can't just lie around here while who knows what is happening all around us!"

"Oh, just relax, Dooley," I muttered, on the verge of tumbling headfirst into sleep.

"Relax! How can I relax when... when…"

But at this point I'd finally found sleep, or maybe sleep had found me? At any rate I'd become blissfully oblivious of Dooley's ramblings. There's only so much angst one can stomach. And it was with extreme reluctance that I pulled myself from the depths of a super slumber when a sharp voice interrupted a sweet dream about a new addition to cat choir, a tabby tease who wasn't merely blessed with great pipes, but was quite the looker to boot.

"Max! Wake up! Something terrible has happened!"

It was Harriet, who's a member of our posse. Immediately, I was up and ready for action. When Dooley is yammering on about all sorts of imaginary threats, I'm not bothered. That's just par for the course. But when Harriet does the same... it means something's up.

"What's wrong?" I didn't even bother rubbing the sleep from my eyes. It's one of the advantages of being a cat: there's never any sleep that needs to be rubbed. One moment we're practically comatose, the next we're shifting into high gear, all at the drop of a hat. Or the flash of a white whisker, as in this case. That's millions of years of evolution for you.

"It's Odelia," said Harriet, a strikingly pretty white Persian. She was slightly panting. With my keen detective's eye, I could tell she'd been running. Or was under duress. Or both.

"Odelia! What's wrong with Odelia?" Dooley practically yelled.

Odelia is our human, and in that sense pretty much our raison d'être one could say. I know, I know. Cats are supposed to be these independent creatures, unattached and unfettered. Don't let our stoic and aloof look fool you, though. We do care about our humans, and we don't like it when something bad happens to them. That's why I was ready to skip sleep and follow Harriet without a moment's hesitation, and so was Dooley.

"What happened to her?" I asked, already fearing the worst.

"Just hurry," said Harriet, and sprinted ahead of us at a high rate of speed. We tore through the backyard, tore through the small strip that separates Odelia's house from her neighbors, and tore out across the front yard. Ours is a corner of the world where people still enjoy living in houses that are detached, semi-detached or even attached. No apartments for us, and a good thing, too. I wouldn't enjoy being an apartment cat.

We were out onto the street and Harriet still showed no signs of slowing down. Already I was breathing heavily. I'm a cat built for cuddles, not for speed. Some people call me portly, but they're wrong, of course. I'm big-boned is what I am. A matter of genetics.

"Where are we going?" I managed between two stertorous intakes of breath.

But Harriet didn't even bother to respond. It just confirmed to me how grave the situation really was. Usually she's the chatterbox of our small clowder of cats, and the fact that she hadn't uttered more than a few words told me this was bad. Very bad indeed.

She tore around the corner and I could tell we were heading for the park, the very place I'd been dreaming about only moments before. Oh, how long ago this now seemed.

"I don't like this, Max," Dooley intimated.

Well, I didn't like it either, but at that point I was too winded to respond. Into the park Harriet zipped, and Dooley and I followed, still going full tilt. We almost bumped into her when she abruptly stopped, and then we just stood there, me panting, she squinting.

"There," she said finally, pointing with her fluffy white tail.

I looked there. And I didn't see a thing.

"What are we looking at?" I asked therefore, scanning the horizon for a sign of a bleeding and grievously harmed Odelia, most probably on the verge of expiration.

"There!" she repeated, this time pointing with her paw.

4

And that's when I saw it. Dooley must have seen it too, for he drew in a sharp breath.

It was Odelia, only she wasn't bleeding. Worse, she was locking lips with a man.

And this man was not—I repeat this man was NOT… her boyfriend Chase Kingsley.

CHAPTER 2

"*M*ax?" asked Dooley, his voice croaky and weird. "What's going on?"

"Can't you see what's going on!" Harriet replied in my stead. "That's our human down there, being treacherous!"

Treacherous was not the word I would have used. As far as I know humans are not a monogamous species. Not unlike cats—though some cats have been known to be loyal to their mate until their dying day. Harriet is not one of those cats, so I found her indignation highly hypocritical. I didn't mention this, though, for Harriet's claws are as sharp as her tongue, and I wasn't looking for a lashing of either. Still, I wouldn't have thought it possible for Odelia to cheat on her boyfriend. I'm not an expert on human love, but I'd had the impression true love was involved in this particular pairing of a reporter and a local copper.

"Max! What's going on?!" Dooley practically wailed.

"I think what's going is that Odelia, being human and therefore flawed, is making an error of judgment,'" I said carefully. Dooley is not one of your tough cats. He's sensitive,

6

and situations like these are something he should be shielded from, not encouraged to witness.

I directed a reproachful glance at Harriet, who should have known better than to subject Dooley to this kind of sordid scene. Of course my glance went right over her head.

"She's enjoying it," said Harriet now.

And she was right. Odelia clearly was enjoying this romantic interlude with one who was not her chosen mate.

"I don't like this, Max," said Dooley, not taking this well. "I don't like this at all."

"I don't like it either," I intimated, "but such is life, Dooley. Sometimes the people we think we know best surprise us. And not always in a good way."

Just then, a third person approached Odelia and the unknown male, and spoke a few words. The effect of these was immediate. Odelia extricated herself from her kissing partner and got up from the picnic blanket on which she'd been sitting. She stood, hands on hips, while this third person, another male, seemed to explain something to her. Possibly giving her pointers on her kissing technique.

The scene, apart from the shock effect it had on those who'd become used to seeing Odelia linked in body and soul to Chase Kingsley, was otherwise a peaceful and idyllic one: there was a picnic basket present, a picnic table, and even a dog lying at the lovers' feet.

I did a double take. Wait, what? A dog? Where did this mutt come from? Odelia didn't have a dog. Or did she?

Dooley had spotted the dog, too, for he produced a sound like a kettle boiling.

"Looks like Odelia is moving on," said Harriet, voicing the thought that had occurred to me as well.

"She's getting rid of us and getting... a dog?" I said, now shocked to the core.

"Looks like," Harriet confirmed. "She was petting him before, and he seemed to like it."

I was speechless. Kissing strange men was one thing, but getting a dog to replace her loyal brace of cats? That was too much. No, really! After everything we'd done for her she was getting a dog? This was treason of the highest order. Worse. This was a travesty.

I decided enough was enough, and set paw for the despicable scene.

"Max, no!" Dooley and Harriet cried out, but I paid them no heed. Odelia had gone too far, and I was going to speak my mind and tell her what was what, even at the price of having to be within twenty yards of a canine, which was the limit I usually set myself.

When I approached the picnic scene, Odelia was frowning, listening intently to the second, non-kissing male, a man with a fashionable red beard that curled up at the end, as was the current trend. Meanwhile the kisser was munching on a sandwich, not a care in the world.

The dog was the first one to become aware of my impending arrival, for he lifted first his head, then his upper lip in a vicious snarl.

I hesitated, but decided this mission was too important to be derailed by the pathetic snarls of a cat's mortal enemy.

"Odelia!" I said, deciding to come in strong and pitch my sentiments before she had a chance to become distracted by her lover and the bearded hipster dude.

Odelia looked up, that frown still furrowing her forehead.

"A word, please?" I said, keeping a keen eye on the canine, whose upper lip was trembling now, his eyes shooting menace and all manner of mayhem in my direction.

"Max!" said Odelia, clearly surprised to see me. She quickly shut up. It's not a fact widely known, but Odelia belongs to a long line of women who talk to cats. From generation to generation, this gift is passed, and a good thing, too. For far too long, humans have turned a deaf ear to a cat's desires. Now, with Odelia and her mother and gran to listen to our plea, our voice is no longer ignored. Who also wasn't ignoring my voice was the dog.

"What do you want, cat?" he snarled, his hind legs tensing as he got ready to pounce.

"This doesn't concern you, Lassie," I said, holding up my paw. "So back off."

"This is my terrain, cat," he shot back, tail wagging dangerously. "Get lost or else."

"Or else what?" I asked, sounding a lot braver than I was feeling. Those fangs did not look appealing. Saliva was dripping from them, and already thoughts of rabies and front-page articles about a blorange cat being mauled to death started popping into my mind.

"You don't want to find out," he said with a low growl that seemed to rise up straight from his foul innards.

Odelia, who'd followed the tense interaction, crouched down next to me. "Max," she said quietly, so the kisser and the hipster couldn't overhear. "What are you doing here?"

"I could ask you the same thing," I said, as haughtily as I could. "I saw you," I added. "Canoodling with that... that... man."

Odelia frowned, as if not comprehending what I was saying. Then, suddenly, she laughed! Actually burst out laughing! "Oh, Max," she said, giving my head a patronizing pet. "That's just acting!"

"Whatever it is, it's despicable," I said. Then I frowned. "What do you mean, acting?"

She gestured with her head to the kisser, who now stood chatting with the weird red beard. "That's Don Stryker. He's a New York stage actor. And the man with the beard is Wolf Langdon—he's our director."

And then I remembered. Odelia had mentioned something about performing in something called Bard in the Park, and had even mentioned snagging an important role.

I stared her. "You mean this is all... acting?"

"All of it," she assured me, then took an apple from the picnic basket and took a bite, plunking down next to me. She lowered her voice. "And let me tell you, it's no picnic so far. This guy's breath..." She rolled her eyes and waved a hand in front of her face. "Hoo-wee."

In spite of myself I laughed. "Garlic. I can smell it a mile away. I thought you liked it."

"No, Max. Women don't like it when men chew a clove of garlic before a big kissing scene. Allegedly that's how Clark Gable annoyed Vivien Leigh in *Gone with the Wind*."

I decided to skip the small talk. I hadn't forgotten about my real beef. "What about that," I said, pointing at the rabid dog, still snarling and softly growling in my direction.

"Scoochie?" she said. "He's in the scene. He's an actor, too."

"The dog is an actor?"

"Sure. Dogs can be actors. Pretty much any animal can be an actor."

This was news to me. Slightly mollified, I asked the most important question of all: "So... He's not going to live with us?"

Odelia laughed again and patted my head. "Silly Max. Of course not. He's going home with his trainer once rehearsals are over. And right now he lives with the rest of the troupe at Whitmore Manor. In his own room. Did you think I'd adopt a dog and not tell you guys?"

"No, of course not," I said, "Don't be silly." But behind her back I gave Harriet and Dooley, who still sat watching from a safe distance, two thumbs up. Or rather, since cats don't have those nifty and very handy opposable thumbs, two claws up at any rate.

"Hey, what's wrong with adopting a dog?" growled the dog.

"Nothing," Odelia was quick to say.

That's how my human is: kind to animals, children and even dogs.

"I thought so," grumbled the mutt.

The man Odelia had identified as the director now turned to her. "I liked what you did there, dahling," he said, "but could you give it a little more—I don't know—oomph?"

"Oh, sure," said Odelia, getting up. "What sort of oomph are we talking about here?"

She began discussing the ins and outs of the oomphs of acting in detail, and I soon lost interest. Instead, I glanced around and saw that a small film crew sat hiding behind a nearby tree. They'd filmed the whole thing! Probably to learn from and correct later.

I just hoped they hadn't filmed Odelia and me chatting. Because that would definitely not be good!

CHAPTER 3

*O*delia watched Max stalk off, his tail in the air, his rear end wagging slightly, and couldn't help but smile. She could only imagine what he must have thought when he saw her kissing Wolf Langdon like that. In the distance, she saw Dooley and Harriet, anxiously awaiting Max's return with news from the front line. Cats were sensitive creatures, who hated change. Kissing a strange man must have spooked them a great deal. Just then, her real-life boyfriend appeared, crossing the plain to where she stood. Don, who'd been snacking on the contents of the picnic basket, saw him coming and a dark cloud seemed to descend over him. "Don't tell me Captain America is going to cause trouble," he said.

"Chase isn't here to cause trouble," Odelia said. She didn't much care for her co-star. Apart from his garlic antics, he was arrogant and not much fun to be around. And he had a habit of sticking his tongue down her throat, even though it wasn't part of the script.

Chase had joined them and gave Odelia a quick peck on the lips. "Hey, babe," he said in that low rumbling voice of his.

He held out a hand to shake Don's, but the actor simply ignored him and walked away, a dirty look on his otherwise handsome face.

"See ya around, Poole," Don muttered, and was off.

Chase retracted the hand. "What was that all about?"

"Oh, nothing. Don has this thing about the boyfriends of his leading ladies."

Chase quirked an eyebrow. "A thing? What thing?"

"He was once on the receiving end of a punch thrown by an actress's spouse. His nose has never been the same."

"He must have given him reason," said Chase, looking on as Don made his way over to the makeup table for a touch-up and a flirtatious chat with the makeup ladies.

"I'd say he did," said Odelia. "Don Stryker has a reputation as a ladies' man, and he likes to make sure that reputation stays earned."

Chase quirked his other eyebrow. "Should I worry about this Stryker guy?"

She smiled. "No, of course not." She draped her arms around his neck and gave him a kiss. "Nothing to worry about at all."

"That's more like it," he rumbled, then lifted her up into a full-body hug. If Don was watching, the hug might be inter-preted as a gesture of possessiveness but Odelia didn't care. There was only one man in her life and that was Chase, and no arrogant Broadway star could change that.

"So I was thinking," said Chase now.

"Yes?"

"I was thinking we haven't gone out on a date in a while—just you and me."

She liked where this was going. "So what do you suggest?"

"I suggest dinner and a movie? There's a new place in Happy Bays we haven't tried. It's called The Dusty Tavern and they're rumored to serve some damn fine clam chowder."

"The Dusty Tavern it is, then."

"I have some stuff to finish up at the precinct. Pick you up at the house at seven?"

"Sounds great. See you later, Chase."

"See you, babe," he said with a happy grin, then was off, but not before giving Don the kind of look that would remind him of the punch that had given his nose that tweak.

Odelia sank down on the blanket and took the script she'd tucked underneath the basket and opened it to a well-thumbed page. This was the first time she was playing a part in a play, or any performance, for that matter. She had no acting experience whatsoever, but she didn't mind. It wasn't as if this production would be seen by more than a few people.

Bard in the Park was a strictly local setup, designed to entertain natives and tourists alike. Not exactly the start of a great career in acting. More like a fun way to while away the time and do something different for a change. Also, Dan Goory, her editor at the Hampton Cove Gazette, had instructed her to write a piece on the acting troupe, and the recurrent phenomenon of summer public theater, and what better way to write about Shakespeare in the Park than to immerse herself in its world and even play a small part?

She frowned as she read through her lines. The hardest part about this acting thing was memorizing those big chunks of text. She was constantly in fear she would drop a line and get absolutely, completely stuck, with people all staring at her. Which was why she was determined to study hard and nail her dialogues until she could recite them in her sleep.

And she was still muttering William Shakespeare's memorable and immemorial lines to herself when a loud scream suddenly pierced the air. She looked up, startled, and was even more surprised when she saw a small group of people standing around nearby, the director and some of the other troupe members among them.

She got up and hurried over, afraid someone had become unwell and had collapsed.

When she reached the small throng Wolf Langdon, his face white as a sheet, was already clutching his phone to his ear and barking, "She's dead. She's dead, I'm telling you!"

Finally Odelia reached the commotion. On the ground, her face frozen in a mask of shock, a young woman lay motionless, her eyes staring unseeingly up at the people all crowding around her. It wasn't hard to figure out she was, indeed, dead, what with the big knife sticking out of her chest. Odelia recognized her as Dany Cooper. Her understudy.

CHAPTER 4

"*S*o... I don't get it," said Dooley once I'd explained to him and Harriet why Odelia had been kissing this man.

Harriet rolled her eyes, but I cut in before she could launch a scathing comment. "What don't you get, Dooley?"

"So it's all right for humans to cheat on their significant others when the person they're cheating with is an actor? Is that how it works?"

"Oh, Dooley," said Harriet, unable to contain herself. "They weren't really kissing. They were acting!"

"It looked like they were kissing to me," said Dooley.

It looked like that to me, too. "They were only pretending to be kissing," I said. "None of it is real. Like in *Game of Thrones*? When they cut off people's heads, the way they do on that show, the actors still get to walk away when the scene is over. Heads attached."

"Yes, but Odelia has to lock lips with this guy, right?"

"Right," I admitted.

"I mean, it's not CGI like in *Game of Thrones*. It's her

actual lips on this guy's actual lips. And they're actually kissing. Swapping bodily fluids and rubbing tongues and all that."

"You don't have to be so graphic about it," I grumbled.

"No, but I'm right, right?"

"I guess so."

"So what's the difference between a movie kiss and a real kiss?"

Tough question. "Well, for one thing, a real kiss has emotion. Humans kiss each other because they love each other—like Odelia and Chase. This guy, that's not real."

"It looked real to me."

"Yes, well, it's not," said Harriet snappishly. "So just drop it, will you?" She shook her head. "I can't believe I've wasted my time on this nonsense. And I still haven't been able to find Brutus, the reason I came to the park in the first place."

We all looked around, as if fully expecting Brutus to suddenly pop up from behind a bush or a tree.

"I don't know," said Harriet. "I haven't seen him all day. It's not like him to go off without a word."

"Why don't we ask that nice dog over there to sniff him out?" Dooley suggested.

"That nice dog just threatened me," I said. "So he's not a nice dog at all."

"But he is a dog, and dogs are known for their ability to find missing persons—and cats."

We all turned to Scoochie. Dooley wasn't the smartest cat in the world, but even not-so-smart cats get these sudden flashes of insight. Maybe now was Dooley's turn for a flash.

"Are you nuts?" Harriet asked suddenly. "Why ask a dog to do a cat's job? Our sense of smell is superior to that of a dog—didn't you know that?"

"Um…" said Dooley, blinking.

"We have 200 million receptors in our noses, far more than any dog." She tapped Dooley's nose. "So repeat after me. We don't need dogs. To suggest we do is ridiculous."

"We don't need dogs," Dooley muttered meekly.

"We don't need dogs," I echoed.

"But if that's true, why haven't you been able to track down Brutus?" asked Dooley now, risking hide and hair to point out the fatal flaw in Harriet's reasoning.

She narrowed her eyes at him, opened her mouth to speak, then closed it again.

"Dooley has a point," I said, backing up my buddy.

"Hrmph," was Harriet's only response.

Just at that moment, there was a loud commotion nearby. Humans were converging on the scene, and even Odelia hurried to where a small group of other humans stood.

"Uh-oh," I said. "Looks like something's going down down there."

"I don't care," said Harriet. When we turned to her, she explained, "I cared when I thought Odelia was cheating on Chase, because…" She bit her lower lip. "I'm starting to think Brutus is cheating on me." She studied her paws. "There, I said it. Now make fun of me all you want."

"We're not going to make fun of you, Harriet," I said.

"Yeah, we're your friends," Dooley chimed in. "We'd never make fun of you."

Except when she was being unreasonable, which was a lot. Or when she was doing her diva thing again, which was also a lot. But apart from that? Never.

"Hey, you guys," a voice sounded behind us. It was Tigger, a member of cat choir who lives near the park. "You gotta see this. Brutus is making out with some hot chick." Then he caught sight of Harriet and gulped then quickly snuck away, clearly fearing her wrath.

"Brutus is making out?" Harriet said between gritted teeth. "Where? Come back here, you little weasel!"

But Tigger was gone. Harriet's eyes were flashing and she quickly retraced Tigger's steps, both Dooley and I following in her wake. It didn't take us long to arrive at the duck pond that's one of the park's main features. Children can usually be found there, gleefully ignoring the big 'DON'T FEED THE DUCKS' sign and feeding the ducks. There's a nice copse of beech trees just across the little bridge that spans the pond. Harriet was already sniffing the air, trying to pick up the scent of her errant mate.

Dooley and I exchanged a glance of worry. If Tigger was right, and Brutus was indeed making out with 'some hot chick,' there would be hell to pay. Not to mention scars to nurse.

Harriet stalked across the bridge, and Dooley and I followed at a little distance. I love Harriet, and she's one of my best friends, but there are times she scares the crap out of me, and this was one of those times.

We'd arrived on the other side of the bridge, and kids were already pointing in our direction and yelling, "Look, mama, kitty catties!"

Those same mamas probably thought we were stalking a duck breeding ground, and judging from the irate looks on their faces were getting ready to chase us away. What they didn't know was that we weren't advancing on a duck breeding ground but apparently on a Brutus breeding ground.

Arriving at the small crop of trees, Harriet sniffed twice, then made a growling sound at the back of her throat. I sniffed, too, and immediately knew we were on the right track. Or the wrong one, depending whose side you were on.

"Brutus!" Harriet bellowed, then made a mighty leap and arrived at the little clearing between the trees.

And there he was, not exactly making out with a hot female feline, but still in flagrante delicto: Brutus, that black, butch cat, was sniffing the butt of a gorgeous redhead.

CHAPTER 5

*B*rutus looked exactly like what he was: busted!

"I, um, I'm…" he stammered, then finally resorted to that old standby: "It's not what it looks like!"

"Oh, puh-lease," said Harriet, and would have folded her front legs across her chest if she'd been human. "Don't give me that crap. Don't tell me you were acting, too."

"Huh?" said Brutus. To his credit, this was not an excuse he'd considered.

The redhead, whom I'd recognized as Darlene, one of cat choir's femme fatales, appeared unruffled. She gave Harriet a faux curious look. "So you're the girlfriend, huh?"

"You know I'm the girlfriend, Darlene," Harriet snapped. "Though not for much longer. In fact I'm officially handing the girlfriend baton to you." She slashed the air with her tail for emphasis, then lifted her chin imperiously. "And I sincerely hope you choke on it." Having delivered this message, she then promptly turned on her heel and stalked off.

Darlene laughed a throaty laugh. She seemed to find the whole thing hilarious.

Brutus was less sanguine. "Sweetums, wait!" he yelled, and would have gone after Harriet if I hadn't stopped him with a gesture of my paw.

"No good?" he asked.

"No good," I returned.

I'd known Harriet practically from the cradle, and when she was in a vengeful mood like this, the only thing that would result in Brutus going after her was fur flying and claws slashing tender skin. I might not have liked Brutus in the past, but close association had warmed me to the butch cat, and I couldn't stand the thought of him having to lick his wounds after a close encounter with Harriet's wrath. The only words appropriate in a situation like this came to me and so I spoke them.

"What the hell were you thinking?!"

"You guys seem to have a lot to talk about so I'll leave you to it," said Darlene. "Toodle-oo." And she sashayed off, every sign of the feline femme fatale in her manner.

The three of us couldn't help but stare after her. I might not be a big fan of cat fatales, but that doesn't mean I can't admire them when I meet one. Finally, she rounded the bend and when no sounds of cats fighting reached my ear, I assumed Harriet hadn't been lying in wait and her rival had gotten to safety unchecked and unharmed.

Once again I turned to Brutus. "What were you thinking?" I repeated.

"Yeah, what were you thinking, Brutus?" Dooley echoed.

Brutus looked devastated. "You have to help me, Max. You have to talk to Harriet."

"All the talking in the world isn't going to help you now, Brutus. You've officially done it."

"But that's just it. I haven't done a thing!" he said, wringing his paws.

I uttered a sound of exasperation. "We saw you! You

were... doing whatever you were doing. In the bushes! The cliché to end all clichés!"

"Officially this is not a bush. It's a thicket," Dooley corrected me.

"I wasn't doing anything! I was never going to let it go that far."

"You had your nose up Darlene's butt, Brutus."

"I hadn't!"

"Well, from where I was standing it looked like you had."

"A matter of perspective. My nose wasn't anywhere near her butt!"

"Who cares where your nose was?! You were in the bushes! Making out!"

"Thicket," said Dooley, then shut up when I gave him a foul look.

Brutus plunked down on his haunches, a look of distress in his dark eyes. "I know how bad this looks, but... have you never been in a long-term relationship and started to wonder?"

Since I'd never been in a long-term relationship, or a short-term one, I wisely kept my tongue.

"Sometimes you just wonder if you've still got it, you know?"

"No, I don't know. What are you talking about?"

"Yes, what are you talking about, Brutus?" Dooley said, looking as puzzled as I was feeling. "Harriet is the finest cat for miles around. How can you cheat on her?"

Dooley had a point. Harriet *was* the finest cat for miles around. What's more, Dooley had always had a thing for Harriet, so this whole Darlene thing came as a shock to him, too.

Brutus raised a helpless paw. "You wonder if you still have it."

"Have what?" I asked.

"It! The pizzazz. The fatal attraction."

"I don't get it," I said, in case that wasn't obvious from the confused look on my map.

Brutus sighed. "I used to be a big thing before, you know. Cats would fawn over me. I'd strut my stuff and heads would turn. I was the Tom Brady of cats, all eyes on me. Queens wanted to be with me—tomcats wanted to be me. I was top cat. Leader of the pack. Head of the herd. Now, no cat looks at me twice, because they know I'm with Harriet. So they don't even bother. It's like I've become invisible, all of a sudden. Not worth their while."

I hardly would have called Brutus, a buff black cat, invisible, but that just goes to show that you can never know another cat's mind. "You're not invisible, Brutus," I said.

"No, I see you, Brutus," Dooley concurred.

These words didn't seem to do much to buck the butch cat up, though. If possible, he slumped even more. "Look, I love Harriet with all my heart—she's the only cat for me. But sometimes a fellow just wants to know if he hasn't lost it, you know? So when Darlene suggested I meet her in the bushes—thicket—I jumped at the chance. I guess I was flattered. Happy that my fatal charm still worked. And it did! Only it worked a little too well, I guess."

"You were sniffing her butt, Brutus," I said.

"I wasn't! Honestly! I would never cheat on Harriet. You know that, Max."

I did know that, but I also knew things looked bad for Brutus. Very bad.

"You gotta help me, Max," he said now, a pleading note in his voice. "You gotta explain to Harriet. Make things right. I can't lose her. I'm nothing without that cat. Nothing!"

"I don't know, Brutus. I know Harriet, and she's not the forgiving kind."

"Oh, man," he moaned. "I've really done it this time, haven't I?"

And with these words, he slunk off in the direction of the pond. For a moment I expected to hear a plunge and was already bracing myself to jump in after him to save his life. No plunging sound came, though, and the moment passed. I should have known. Even in the depths of despair, Brutus wasn't the kind of cat to take his own life. Probably because he knows he'd have to repeat the procedure nine times, and who wants to be bothered?

"What are we going to do, Max?" asked Dooley.

"First we're going to give Harriet a little time to cool off," I said.

"And then we're going to talk to her? Convince her Brutus wasn't really cheating on her? That he was doing exactly what Odelia was doing: playing make-believe?"

I smiled at Dooley's quick insight. "That's exactly what we're going to do. We're going to play Cupid, Dooley."

"It's going to be tough."

"Yes, it is. But when have we ever turned away from a challenge?"

"Never."

I eyed him appreciatively. "Any other cat would have jumped at the chance to use this opportunity to seduce Harriet—become her shoulder to cry on and move in on her."

Dooley looked sincerely shocked. "No way! Harriet loves Brutus and he loves her. I would never do that to two of my best friends."

"You know what, Dooley? You just might be one of the most chivalrous cats around."

He looked confused. "What's chivalrous, Max?"

"You, Dooley. You are chivalrous. A regular knight of old." These words didn't seem to mean a thing to my friend, so I added, "You're a true friend. Now let's go and check out this hullaballoo. I do believe Odelia just may have stumbled upon yet another murder."

"She should probably stop doing that. It's a very bad habit."

CHAPTER 6

"Who was she?" asked Uncle Alec.

Odelia was seated on a bench, still experiencing the kind of dread that accompanies the discovery of a fellow human being whose life has been snuffed out prematurely.

"Her name was Dany Cooper."

"I don't think I've seen her around," said Alec, glancing in the direction of the crime scene, which his officers had cordoned off and where the coroner was now conducting his investigations.

"She's not from around here. We haven't exchanged more than a few words but I think she's from Albany, though she's been living in New York for the past couple of months, with aspirations of becoming an actress on the stage."

And now someone had murdered her. Just like that. In broad daylight, with dozens of witnesses around. Odelia shook her head. "I don't get it. Someone must have seen something, right? This kind of thing can't just... happen."

"We're still talking to anyone who was in the vicinity," the Chief assured her.

And now he was talking to her. Not in his capacity as her uncle, but as the chief of police. She was a witness, after all. It felt a little weird being in this position. Usually she was the one asking the questions. This time, tragedy had struck close to home. She watched as her cats came trotting up. Careful, as if not wanting to disturb her. She didn't see Brutus or Harriet, though. Just Max and Dooley. She smiled down at them as they took up their position underneath the bench, eavesdropping on her the way they eavesdropped on all humans. Cats were the ultimate detectives: nobody ever noticed them, or if they did, they didn't care. So they heard stuff—stuff that wasn't intended for anyone's ears. This way Odelia had solved quite a few mysteries. She hoped she'd be able to solve this one, too.

"So what was her role, exactly?" asked Alec.

"She was supposed to learn my part, in case anything happened to me, so she could take over and allow the production to go on."

"Do you think the production will go on now? I mean, this is a pretty tragic event."

"I haven't talked to Wolf yet."

"Wolf?"

"Wolf Langdon. He's the director. He's been running these Bard in the Park productions for years, setting them up all across the state. He's a big name on Broadway, but his summers are spent showcasing Shakespeare in small towns like Hampton Cove. His way of introducing the bard—and theater—to the masses." And discovering local talent.

She watched as Chase interviewed Don Stryker. She could have told him he was wasting his time. Don was notoriously self-absorbed. He wouldn't have noticed someone as low on the totem pole as Dany Cooper. Not important enough to cozy up to, and not attractive enough for a quick roll in the hay, and therefore negligible. Besides, he had a perfect alibi: he'd been over by the craft services table, chatting up one of the interns.

"Was she killed at that exact spot?" asked Odelia. "Under that tree?"

"Looks like," said Alec.

"But how is that even possible? She was in full view of everyone."

"Not really. From what I can gather they were all so focused on you and this Stryker guy they didn't bother to turn around. Otherwise they would have noticed how one of their own was being murdered right behind them."

"But we were taking a break. Don was over by the craft services table and I was…" She lowered her voice. "… talking to Max."

Uncle Alec shrugged. It was obvious how he felt about the crew's powers of observation.

Odelia gestured to one of the cameramen. "They're filming this whole thing. Not just the rehearsals but the entire process. Wolf hopes to turn it into a documentary. Maybe they caught the killer on tape?"

"We're going to sift through every inch of film," said Alec, making a note in his little notebook.

"Maybe someone else saw something?" She pointed to a mother pushing a stroller on a pathway that curved around a grassy slope that stretched between their rehearsal spot and the duck pond. "That path over there offers a perfect vantage point to see the tree."

Uncle Alec let his reading glasses dangle from his neck and fixed her with his mellow brown eyes. They were slightly hooded, which gave him a hangdog look. "We're working on it, honey. I've got all my people combing through the park. Don't you worry. We'll get whoever did this. They won't get away with it."

She nodded. His words offered a measure of comfort,

though she couldn't help but fret over the whole thing. "Somehow I have the feeling I'm responsible," she said suddenly.

"That doesn't make any sense. How are you responsible for what happened to Dany?"

"Because she was my understudy. If not for me…"

"If not for you, she would have been someone else's understudy. This has nothing to do with you," he said, and he was right. It didn't stop her from feeling terrible about the whole thing.

"I don't know," she said, shaking her head. "Somehow this feels… personal."

"How so?" asked Uncle Alec with a frown.

"I don't know—but it just does."

"Trust me when I tell you this wasn't personal, Odelia. So don't you go blaming yourself now, you hear?" She nodded, and looked up when her uncle suddenly muttered, "Holy crap."

"What is it?"

He was looking at his phone, then held it up so she could see. "Picture of the murdered girl. Notice anything?"

She stared at the picture of Dany Cooper and smiled a wan smile. "She was beautiful."

"She was," Uncle Alec confirmed. "She was also the spitting image… of you."

CHAPTER 7

I didn't like all this talk about people resembling Odelia being murdered. I mean, if humans want to kill each other, that's perfectly fine with me, but please don't touch MY human. She's off-limits. And so are the members of my human's family, for that matter.

"I don't like this, Dooley," I said therefore.

Dooley stared at me dumbly. This was his line, and I'd just blatantly stolen it.

"I don't get it," he said.

Now that was a line I wasn't ready to steal, as I got it just fine. "A woman has just been murdered and she was the spitting image of Odelia," I explained.

"Oh, I don't like that, Max," he said. Then he thought about this some more and said, "I still don't get it. Why would anyone murder a woman just because she looks like Odelia?"

I hitched up my shoulders in a shrug. "That, I don't know," I admitted. I mean, we all know humans are weird, and there's often no rhyme or reason to what they do. This seemed like another case in point.

"Are you saying there's someone going around murdering Odelia's lookalikes?" Dooley pressed on.

"We won't know for sure until he kills his second Odelia lookalike," I said. The moment I spoke the words, I realized how this sounded.

"I hope that doesn't happen, Max," said Dooley, echoing my thoughts exactly.

And judging from the shocked look on Odelia's face, who was being interviewed on the bench right above our heads by Uncle Alec, she was thinking the exact same thing.

"Chances are this is just a coincidence," Alec was saying.

Odelia nodded numbly. "I'm sure you're right. Just a horrible coincidence." She stared at her uncle's phone some more. "I never realized before how closely she resembled me. Or how closely I resembled her. We could have been sisters." She frowned. "So that's why Wolf chose her. Not just because she was a great actress but because we're like twins."

"At any rate," said Uncle Alec, tucking away his little note-book and heaving his bulk from the bench with a groan, "I can assure you we'll get to the bottom of this. And you better take the rest of the day off."

"I can't," she said. "I still have an article to write for the Gazette."

"Not about the murder, surely," said Alec, incredulous.

"The moment Dan found out about it, he reserved space on tomorrow's front page. I need to get my piece in by six tonight so he can still make his edits."

"Can't he write the piece himself? You're in no state of mind to write about this. Too close to home," he explained.

"I'll be fine, Uncle Alec," she said, giving him a brave smile. "I've handled worse. Remember when Mom was a murder suspect?"

"This is different," Alec said, and he was right. "I think

you better sit this one out, honey. I'll tell Chase not to involve you, either."

"But..."

He held up a meaty paw. "No buts about it. I have a bad feeling about this, and I wouldn't be much of a cop if I didn't follow my gut from time to time." He slapped his voluminous belly. "God knows it's big enough not to ignore. You're not to get involved in this case and that's my final word."

Odelia looked mutinous, but knew better than to argue with her uncle. They're both cut from the same cloth and if there was ever a competition for obstinate mules, it would be a photo finish.

"Fine," she said finally, but without much enthusiasm.

Dooley pointed to Odelia's back. "Why is she crossing her fingers, Max?"

"That's what humans do when they say one thing but plan to do the exact opposite."

Dooley shook his head. "Humans are so weird."

"Tell me about it."

Uncle Alec left to join his people and Odelia turned to us. "Listen, you guys. We need to figure out who killed Dany. You're going to be my eyes and ears on this one, all right?"

"All right," I said, nodding earnestly.

"I'll be your ears and Max can be your eyes," said Dooley happily.

"Um.... fine," said Odelia.

"And Brutus can be your nose and Harriet can be your tongue," Dooley continued.

"Dooley," I said warningly.

"And Kingman can be your..." Dooley frowned. "Um, what other sense is there?"

"Touch—but that's not important," I said. I turned to Odelia. "We'll all be your eyes and ears and whatever else you need. Rest assured, we'll nab this nasty killer for you."

NIC SAINT

"Oh, and make sure Uncle Alec doesn't find out," she added. "I'm not supposed to participate in this particular investigation."

I tapped my nose with my paw. "Don't worry. Mum's the word."

Odelia went off in the direction of the park exit, and I realized Dooley was staring at me. "Why did you do that thing with your nose, Max? And why is mom the word?"

"It's an expression," I said, already plotting our next course of action. Detection work is a highly specialized business, and by now I was getting to be an old hand at the thing.

"But why mom?" Dooley insisted. "Why not dad's the word? Or grandma's the word? They're nice words. Definitely as nice as mom."

"It's not mom—it's mum. Mum's the word."

"What's a mum?"

"A British mom."

"But why?"

"I don't know, Dooley. It's just one of those things."

"Why not grandpa or uncle or aunt or cousin or nephew or—"

"We need to talk to the ducks," I said, cutting off Dooley's stream of eloquence.

"Ducks?" he asked, looking up in alarm. "Why ducks?"

"Because this place is full of ducks," I said, pointing to a piece of particularly smelly duck poop park cleaners had overlooked. "So one of them is bound to have seen something."

"I don't like ducks," Dooley intimated.

Trouble was, ducks didn't like us, either. So how were we going to win their trust—enough for them to give us their undivided attention—not to mention critical information?

There was only one way: we'd have to be subtle.

Good thing subtle is a cat's middle name.

CHAPTER 8

Oddly enough, Brutus was still where we'd left him: seated near the thicket of beech trees that were now the silent witnesses to his crime of adultery—or, in Brutus's reading, the crime of wanting to see if his fatal attraction still held sway. When we arrived, he looked up, a gleam of hope in his eyes. "And? What did she say?" he asked.

"That the murdered girl looks just like her, and not to tell Uncle Alec," Dooley returned promptly, causing Brutus to shoot him a look of confusion.

"Huh?" he said.

"I think Brutus was referring to Harriet, not Odelia," I said. And for the sake of our suffering friend, I added, "We haven't talked to Harriet yet. There's been a murder in the park, and Odelia wants us to find out who did it."

"Oh," said Brutus, deflating. It was obvious he didn't care about murder now that his love life was in a shambles.

"We're going to talk to the ducks," Dooley announced. "Even though we don't like ducks, we're going to suck it up for Odelia's sake. And we're going to be subtle about it."

"Well put," I complimented my friend. "First we need a plan of campaign…"

"I'll do it," said Brutus, still sounding morose. "Ducks like me. They know I'm a kindred spirit."

I highly doubted this, but who was I to rain on Brutus's parade? He was down in the dumps, and this could buck him up. Besides, he was as much a feline sleuth as the rest of us.

"But only on one condition," Brutus said, pushing himself up from the spot where he'd dropped after watching Harriet shove off in a huff.

"What's that?" I asked, hoping it wasn't my entire week's supply of Cat Snax. I was willing to do a lot for my human, but I drew the line at sacrificing my favorite snack.

"You're going to talk to Harriet the first chance you get, and you're going to make her forgive me for my mistake."

"I don't know if I can guarantee the last part," I said. "But I'm definitely going to talk to Harriet on your behalf." Once she'd had a minute to simmer down. Or a couple of weeks.

"Deal," said Brutus, then drew himself up to his full height and walked out of the protective cover provided by the thicket and out into the open.

I have to admit I was curious to find out what he meant by the phrase, 'Ducks know I'm a kindred spirit.' Cats and ducks don't have all that much in common. Apart from the fact that we are about the same size—or at least most cats. I'm a little bigger. In fact two ducks can easily fit into my frame. But that's because I have big bones—something we've already discussed—and I'm okay with that. It's a blessing and a curse, as Mr. Monk would say.

Brutus, meanwhile, was making a beeline for a group of ducks, lazing about on the edge of the pond. The ducks, now aware of the arrival of a feline, were making soft quacking sounds, then, when Brutus made no sign of changing course, they all plunged into the pond as one duck, and quickly paddled to a part where Brutus couldn't possibly reach them.

"Ducks!" Brutus yelled from the shoreline. "I come in peace!"

But they weren't having it. They kept darting annoyed and frankly hostile glances at the black cat, and made no attempts to enter into communication with him.

"I know some of my people have in the past behaved atrociously towards some of your people!" he bellowed. "But I'm not like that! I may look like a dangerous predator to you, but I'm also just a cat, standing in front of a duck, asking him to help him!"

Nothing doing, though. As moving as his speech was— with some parts sounding awfully familiar somehow—the ducks weren't budging.

"Tell them about the kindred spirit thing!" I shouted.

Brutus held up his paw in response. "Ducks. I know I'm a cat, but it may surprise you to know that I'm also an honorary duck. That's right. I can swim like a duck! Yes, I can!"

Dooley and I exchanged a puzzled glance. "What is he talking about?" I said.

"I think he's saying he can swim like a duck."

"That's what it sounded like to me. Doesn't he know that cats don't swim?"

"Maybe nobody ever told him?"

We both looked on, the spectacle taking on the entertainment value of a major car crash. You know how it is. It's hard to look away.

The ducks were moving about restlessly. They might not have deigned to respond to Brutus's ramblings, but they'd certainly understood every last word of what he was saying. And the part about being able to swim was clearly causing them considerable concern.

Brutus looked over to where Dooley and I were still officiating the role of his ringside audience, and gave us another paw up. I gave him a paw up back.

"He's going to drown," said Dooley.

"Better get ready to call for help," I said.

Brutus put one paw into the pond, then the next, and soon he was up to his chest in the murky water. A nearby frog gave him a weird look, then hopped off. Probably to get his buddies. This they had to see.

"See?" Brutus shouted to the ducks. "I'm a real duck! I can swim!"

He must have stepped into a hole, though, for suddenly he disappeared, only to return spluttering and sputtering above the surface.

"Help!" he screamed. "I can't swim!"

"I knew it," said Dooley. "Are you going to save him or am I?"

Only trouble was, neither of us could swim either.

Meanwhile Brutus was going under for the third time...

CHAPTER 9

$\mathcal{C}$hase, who was interviewing witnesses, suddenly found his attention snagged by a disturbance taking place near the duck pond. A frown marred his handsome and exceedingly masculine face, and he looked over. The sight that met his eyes surprised him, to say the least. Two cats were seated on the side of the pond, mewling at the top of their lungs. Meanwhile a third cat had stumbled into the water and was in a situation of clear and present danger. Chase, who instantly recognized the cats as—reading from left to right—Max, Dooley and Brutus, wasted no time pondering hows and whys, immediately dropped his note-book, and broke into a 100-meter dash that would have made Usain Bolt proud.

Without a second's hesitation, he jumped headfirst into the pond and disappeared beneath the water's surface. With a few powerful strokes of his arms he reached the spot where he'd last seen Brutus, and then he was diving down into the murky depths. This was Odelia's cat, and if it drowned she'd be devastated. He could not allow that to happen.

He opened his eyes and frantically searched about. But

apart from a few reeds and other dwellers of the deep, he saw no sign of a black cat. He rose to the surface, took a big deep gulp of breath, then went under again, this time scanning closer to the edge of the pond. And then he saw the little bugger: Brutus was floating near the sandy bottom.

He grabbed the poor animal and pushed himself off towards the surface, holding him up like that weird painted monkey holding up the lion cub in *The Lion King*. Elton John didn't break into song when he finally emerged, but Max and Dooley did. Or at least they broke into jubilant praise.

Chase carefully placed Brutus on the bank of the pond and to his elation the black cat, who now looked more like a drowned rat than his usual debonair self, coughed up about a gallon of water, then piteously meowed something only cats were equipped to understand. His two little friends were still meowing up a storm, and not for the first time Chase found himself thinking how great it would be if he could actually understand them.

Odelia, who must have been alerted to the drama that was unfolding, came running. "Oh, my sweet, sweet Brutus!" she cried, concern lacing her voice. "What happened?"

"Beats me," said Chase. "I guess he accidentally fell into the water."

To his surprise, her words apparently hadn't been directed at him but at Max and Dooley, who meowed something in response.

Weird. Almost as if they could understand what she was talking about.

Onlookers had arrived, and were all rubbernecking to their heart's content. It wasn't murder this time but a cat in peril but that didn't stop them from taking out their damn smartphones and filming the heck out of the scene.

Chase ground his teeth. "Put those phones away!" he bellowed, getting up.

He hated this habit of people to film any disaster scene they encountered. Used to be that people actually showed up at the scene of an accident to help out. Now they just wanted to film the whole thing so they could post it on their social media.

"I swear to God," he grumbled. "I'm going to bust some heads."

But Odelia's slender fingers enveloped his bicep and she said, "Thank you so much, Chase. You're my hero."

His anger melted like snow before a blistering sun and when she hugged him to show her gratitude, his mind went momentarily blank. When she pulled back, he said, "Oh, Christ. I've made you all wet." Her blouse, her jeans... She was almost as soaking wet as he was.

"I don't mind," she said, a smile lighting up her face.

He knew those cats of hers meant the world to her, and he was glad he'd been there to save Brutus. If he'd been even one minute late in responding...

Oddly enough, a small flock of ducks now came floating up, quacking softly. They waddled onto the shore and approached Brutus, first hesitantly, then with more gusto. And then the weirdest thing happened: the ducks quacked, and Brutus meowed. Almost as if they were communicating! Crazy, of course, but then such was life down here in Hampton Cove. As close to a regular Garden of Eden as humanly possible, complete with talking animals. He shook off the thought. Murder and mayhem didn't happen in the Garden of Eden, but they sure happened in this adopted town of his too often to be dismissed.

"You better go change," said Alec, who'd also joined them. "Or else you'll catch a cold. Here." He shrugged off his light sports jacket and handed it to Chase. "Remove your shirt and put this on."

"I'm fine," he said.

"That's an order, Detective Kingsley," said the Chief, warningly raising an eyebrow.

Grudgingly, he removed his shirt. As he did, there were gasps from their small audience, and women all along the shoreline gripped their smartphones even more intently than before.

Odelia grinned. "Careful, Chase. You don't want to cause a scene."

"Yeah, Chase," Alec echoed. "Disturbing the peace. I'll have to caution you."

"You don't caution the town hero who just saved a cat from drowning, boss," said Chase, shrugging into his superior officer's jacket. It was several sizes too big but it was warm and dry. "If you do, then you'll cause a disturbance."

Alec took in the swooning women. "I guess you're right. At least take the man's picture, Odelia."

"Why?" asked Odelia, puzzled.

"For your story! For God's sakes, woman. Are you a reporter or not? I can see the headline now. Hero Cop Saves Drowning Cat." He clapped Chase on the shoulder. "This is the stuff of legend, son. You're in the town annals now."

"I'm just glad the little fellow is all right," said Chase, giving Brutus a gentle stroke along his fur. Odelia had wrapped him up in her own sweater but he was still shivering violently. "Better take him to the vet," he suggested, and he could have sworn that at the mention of the word 'vet,' all three cats started screaming bloody murder.

CHAPTER 10

*W*hile Chase was showing off his manly humps and bumps to an adoring crowd of ladies, I was recovering from the shock of watching one of my best friends almost end up in a watery grave.

"How are you, Brutus?" I asked.

He looked dazed, and nor did I wonder. If I'd been in his paws, I'd have looked dazed, too.

"I don't think I'm an honorary duck," he said finally.

"No, I could see that."

"Good thing Chase was there to save you," said Dooley.

We all looked up at the hero savior with admiration written all over our features. This wasn't the first time Chase had had to save one of us. The last time it had been me, and Chase had rescued me from a ledge. I'd had an epiphany, then. Chase, with his long hair and masculine features, was nothing short of a come-again Jesus. Dooley actually believed he really was Jesus. The only thing missing was his sheep, but Chase had probably ditched his trusty barnyard animal for a Ford pickup truck. Even Jesus has to keep up with the times.

"The man is a miracle worker," said Brutus reverently. "I didn't believe you that time when you said he was Jesus, Dooley, but now I see you were right. He's an amazing human."

"And he's your human," I reminded Brutus.

"Not really. My real human is Chase's mom, though now I consider your human my human."

I know. It gets complicated. That's because humans have a habit of passing their pets around like candy. A bad habit. Lucky for us Odelia is not like that. She's already told us more than once that she's our human for life, and I believe her. She's one of those rare humans who keep their word, and who truly love their pets.

To my surprise, a small flock of ducks now waddled up onto shore and approached us. One duck hesitantly drew away from the pack. "When you said you could swim, I thought you were kidding," said this duck. Judging from her feathers she was not only the spokesperson but also the leader of the pack. Though truth be told, I'm not an expert on ducks. "But you weren't. You're an amazing swimmer," the duck continued.

"I am?" Brutus asked, surprised.

"Sure. The way you dove right to the hidden depths of this here pond of ours, and went in search of those tasty water bugs that like to lurk in the muck below..." She raised her eyes heavenward. "Amazing. How did you know that was where the best snacks were located?"

"I, um..."

"And you managed to snag two and haven't even consumed them yet," she said, gesturing with her beak to two water beetles happily frolicking on Brutus's belly.

"Aargh!" he said, then quickly brushed them off with a flick of his paw.

They landed right in front of the duck, who stared from the beetles to Brutus. "May I, sir?" she asked, almost reverently.

"Sure. Go ahead. I, um, I'm not hungry."

The duck gobbled up the beetles with a crunching sound —a horrible sight. "Thanks," she said, after heaving a soft burp. "I appreciate it, Duck Burt."

"Brutus," Brutus corrected her.

"On behalf of our community," said the duck, "I want to bid you welcome in our home, Duck Burt. Our pond is your pond. Our bugs are your bugs." She then glanced at Dooley and I. "Are these your friends?"

"Yep. Max and Dooley. My best friends in all the world."

The duck nodded in our direction. "You're most welcome, too. Though the fat one should probably restrain himself. This is a small pond, and there are only so many bugs to go around."

It took me a moment to realize she was referring to me. And I was just about to launch into a very vocal protest when I caught Brutus's eye. 'Don't ruin this, Max,' his expression said. 'Just play along. Nice and easy.'

Grudgingly I buried a few choice comments about fat shaming.

"So did you happen to see what happened out there?" Brutus asked, now that the ice was broken and he'd officially been installed as an honorary duck.

"You mean the slaying? Yes, I did happen to see what happened," said the duck, much to my surprise and not inconsiderable excitement.

"So?" asked Dooley, who couldn't contain his glee. "Who did it?"

"Who did what?" asked the duck, looking Dooley up and down. She must have liked what she saw, for she smiled.

Then again, nobody could ever accuse scrawny Dooley of eating more than his fill.

"Who murdered the girl?" I asked.

Her smile vanished. "Please tell the fat one to be more precise," she said, much to Brutus's glee, for he was trying in vain to suppress a giggle.

"A girl was murdered just now," I said icily. "Her name was Dany Cooper. You said you saw what happened. So who was it? Who killed her?" I must have allowed some of my not inconsiderable resentment to suffuse my words, for she visibly stiffened.

"Duck Burt, perhaps you could tell your fat friend that ducks don't respond well to mockery."

"Mockery?" I cried, flapping my paws. "I'm not mocking you."

"You are, sir," said the duck haughtily. "I find your tone offensive."

I clamped my jaws shut. I was starting to dislike this duck.

Brutus said, "Please forgive Max. He hasn't had his breakfast this morning and he gets grumpy. So what can you tell us about the girl being murdered? Did you see the killer?"

The duck pursed her beak. "I did. I didn't get a good look at his face, but it was definitely a human male. He was wearing a yellow parka and sunglasses and a Knicks cap. Then again, you know what it's like. All humans look the same to us."

I could have told her this was not the case, but I wasn't talking to this duck again.

"Anything else you can tell us?" asked Duck Burt.

The duck smiled a sweet smile. "I like your technique. All that splashing around? How did you know it would stir up so many of those delicious snails, slugs and worms? And could you teach us this amazing technique? There is much we can learn from you, Duck Burt."

Brutus opened his mouth to respond, but at that moment Chase spoke those fateful words that send shivers down the spine of every cat the world over: 'Take him to the vet.'

We all wailed in horror and in shock, our honorary duck-hood suddenly forgotten.

CHAPTER 11

"So how exactly did you end up in the water?" asked Odelia.

Brutus, who was riding shotgun because of the fact that he was the patient today, looked sheepish. "I, um, wanted to take down a witness statement from the ducks, and... I guess I must have ventured out too far. Before I knew it, in my enthusiasm, I was sinking."

Odelia gave him a quick sideways glance. "You're a real hero, do you know that, Brutus? You actually risked life and limb to find out who killed poor Dany."

"Thanks," said Brutus, then sneezed not once but five times in quick succession.

Odelia gave him a look of concern. She didn't like the sneezing. But at least he was alive. For a moment, after Chase had fished him out of the pond, she'd feared he was gone, and it had been like a knife through the heart. If anything ever happened to any of her cats... "Good thing Chase was there," she said now. "If not for him..."

"We should have jumped in," said Max ruefully. "I wanted to, but..."

"You can't swim either. I know. If you'd jumped in, Chase would have had to save the both of you."

"Maybe Chase should teach us how to swim," Dooley now piped up. He'd been awfully quiet. Watching his friend almost drown had clearly made a big impression.

Odelia laughed. "I'll have to tell him that. It'll give him a big laugh."

"No, but I mean it," Dooley insisted. "If Brutus had known how to swim, this would never have happened."

"Dooley is right," Max said, nodding. "What if Chase isn't around next time? What if no one is around and we accidentally stumble into the pond?"

"Accidentally being the key word here," Brutus said.

"If we know how to swim, we can save ourselves."

Odelia frowned. "Maybe that's not such a bad idea." She'd never realized just how dangerous that park could be. Certainly at night. She knew about cat's eyes being a lot more powerful than a human's. But they weren't infallible. On a moonless night, things got so dark that even cats wouldn't be able to see where they were going. They might inadvertently stumble into the pond and… She shivered just thinking about it. With the swiftness that is the hallmark of your top reporter, she made a decision. "Let's do it. Let's teach you guys how to swim. Only I don't think Chase is the right person for the job. For one thing, he won't be able to understand you. No, I'll do it. Or, better yet, Mom, Gran and I will do it. Only we'll have to do it someplace where we won't be overheard, or even seen."

"Maybe we could go down to the beach one morning, very early?" Max suggested.

"Better not. Even when there's no wind, those waves will be tough to negotiate for a beginning swimmer. And I don't want you swept out into deeper waters. It has to be a pool. A shallow one." Maybe a bathtub? Her own was too small, though, and so was her mom's.

"There must be private pools we could sneak into," said Max. "The Hamptons is teeming with pools."

That was true. In the course of her work as a reporter for the Gazette she'd seen pools that would have made Esther Williams salivate. "I'll figure it out," she said. "Now tell me again what that funny little duck said."

"Yellow parka—Knicks ball cap—sunglasses," said Brutus dutifully.

"And she's sure it was a man?"

"Pretty sure. Though she wouldn't recognize his face if she saw it."

"Mh. Too bad. Do you think we should take her to a sketch artist?"

Max, Dooley and Brutus shared a glance in the rearview mirror, then shook their heads in unison. "She's not your most reliable witness," said Max.

"What makes you say that? She volunteered the information, didn't she?"

"She also declared Brutus an honorary duck on account of his unique bug-gathering skills," said Max.

"And she called Max fat," Dooley added.

Those were all proof she was an excellent eyewitness. Then again, it was one thing to take a cat to a sketch artist, and pretend Gran or Odelia were actually supplying the witness statement—like they'd done recently—and quite another to take a duck. Although the duck could talk to Max, and Max could join Odelia at the sketch artist. Or they could even take the sketch artist to the pond, and Max could translate the duck's quackings to Odelia, who could relate them to the artist. She sighed. It all seemed fairly unfeasible. Not to mention the sketch artist would probably think she was nuts. Not that this would be a new thing. Many people in

Hampton Cove thought she and her mom and grandma were a little... weird. The reputation of the Poole women as crazy cat ladies was well-established amongst the locals.

"Okay. For now I'll tell Uncle Alec to look for a man dressed in a yellow parka, wearing a Knicks cap and sunglasses."

Which could be anyone. And the killer would have removed the outfit the moment he left the scene. It still boggled the mind anyone would be so brazen to attack a woman in a public place in broad daylight and get away with it.

"Do I really have to see Vena?" asked Brutus for the umpteenth time.

"Yes, you do," she said. "You almost drowned, Brutus. And that water is not clean. Who knows what diseases you picked up. You might have to get shots."

"Shots!" he cried, sitting up.

"Or maybe not. Let's see what Vena says."

"That water was pretty rank," Dooley agreed.

"Ducks poop in the water. Just saying," said Max.

Brutus gulped. "The things I do for my human," he muttered.

She stroked his head. "And your human appreciates it very much. Though next time you might want to be more careful. We don't want to lose you, buddy. Talking about losing—where is Harriet? I haven't seen her all day."

Another shared look in the rearview mirror. "Um..." Brutus began.

"She's home," Max quickly interjected. "Doesn't want to miss quality time with Gran."

"Quality time with Gran," Odelia repeated slowly. That was a first. There was something they weren't telling her. She decided not to press them. Sooner or later they'd come clean.

She stomped her foot down on the gas, and soon they

were hurtling along the road on their way to the vet. She parked right in front of Vena's office and carried Brutus in, while Max and Dooley entered under their own steam. They might not like it, but Vena was a life saver. Literally. Soon she'd checked out Brutus and declared him fit for duty. Apparently even swallowing a gallon of pond muck hadn't put a dent in the butch cat. Brutus clearly was a force to be reckoned with. And then they were cruising for the homestead. It had been a long day and Odelia couldn't wait to be home and put the day's events behind her.

But first she had an article to write. Or, rather, two: one about Dany, and one about Chase's brave rescue mission. It was Dany Cooper she couldn't stop thinking about, though.

And she knew she wouldn't rest until she'd nailed the bastard who killed her.

CHAPTER 12

*G*ran was watching one of her daytime soaps. Duane
Packer, *General Hospital's* head of gynecology, had
just been unmasked as a fraud and a cheat. He'd
never even graduated from high school, his medical knowledge gleaned from textbooks he'd gotten at a garage sale. Not
only was he a fraud, he'd also been wearing a toupee for the
past ten years. One of the nurses had snatched his toupee,
revealing his shiny bald dome. Gran didn't know what was
worse: the knowledge that General Hospital's most popular
gynecologist had been looking up women's vajajays for the
past decade without a license, or the fact that he had no hair.
At any rate, she was glued to the television as Dr. Packer was
arrested by Port Charles's Chief of Police Jeb Strong and was
being outfitted with a nice pair of shiny cuffs, paraded
through the hospital in a long scene, for everyone to see what
a cheat he was.

"Look at that bald pate," muttered Gran. "Look at the way
it reflects the light. My God, what kind of a monster do you
have to be to pretend to have a full head of hair while you're
as bald as Kojak."

53

Next to her, Harriet made a dismissive noise.

"Oh, that's right. You're too young to remember Kojak. Let me tell you, Telly Savalas was a fine specimen. He was bald but he was gorgeous. His baldness made him even sexier. Not like this asswipe Duane Packer," she added, gesturing at the screen.

"Men are scum," Harriet intoned listlessly.

"You're damn right about that," said Gran. She studied her feline couchmate for a moment. "Trouble in paradise, toots?"

Harriet shrugged. "I caught Brutus sniffing another cat's butt. He claims it wasn't what it looked like."

Gran roared with laughter. "A classic! How many times have I heard that before!"

In actual fact she hadn't heard it all that often. Her husband had said it, obviously, when she'd caught him with his pants down boning her best friend Scarlett Canyon. Jack had been bald, too, which might be where her intense dislike for bald men stemmed from. She wasn't going to delve too deeply into the matter. She was, after all, not a frickin' shrink.

"I mean, it wasn't as if they were actually canoodling or anything."

Gran winced. She preferred to keep the mental picture of her cats strictly PC. Her own motto was that if it wasn't something Disney would approve of, she didn't want to know about it. Just imagine Bambi canoodling with Bambo. Or the Lion King with the Lion Queen. Stuff like that was enough to spoil the one thing in her life that remained unspoiled.

"So where is Brutus now?" she asked, without taking her eye from the screen, where Dr. Packer was still being paraded through the hospital, at a snail's pace, subjected to the scorn of the entire staff and a full wing of patients who, for some reason or other, suddenly had gained the capacity to raise themselves from their sickbeds for this special event.

"I don't know and I don't care," said Harriet, intently scrutinizing a nail.

Gran knew better than to persuade Harriet to give Brutus a second chance. She knew for a fact that Brutus and Harriet were mates for life—just like Odelia and Chase. And her own daughter and that moron Tex. Even though she liked to project an image of grating irascibility, Vesta Muffin was a lot more sentimental than she liked to admit. A good love story never failed to bring a tear to her eye. And the love story of Harriet and Brutus was near and dear to her. "So who's the bimbo?" she asked instead.

"Darlene. I've seen her around. She's in cat choir, of course."

"Of course." Cat choir was the hub of Hampton Cove's cat population's social life. Not much singing went on, as far as Gran could ascertain, but a lot of schmoozing and yapping did, much to the neighbors' discontent. "So what are you going to do about it?"

Harriet shrugged. "What can I do? I'd like to bury my claws in his face. Rearrange his features. But then what? It will give me a fleeting moment of satisfaction but his wounds will heal. If there's a god they will turn into vicious, nasty scars, and the world will move on. Brutus will live happily ever after with his redhead bimbo, always providing she doesn't dump him on account of his new facial arrangements, and I'll be left to wonder why."

Christ, Gran thought. Her cats' lives were even more complicated than *General Hospital*. "Forget about Brutus," she said. "There's plenty of good cats for a babe like you."

Her words didn't seem to buck Harriet up. On the contrary. They seemed to darken the cloud that had appeared over her head. "I could always cut his throat when he's sleeping," she said, pondering ways and means as she spoke. "Or I could gut him. Make him drown in his own blood. And then when he's screaming and choking, he'll look into my eyes and know it's me who did that to him. Or I could cut off his—"

"Okay," said Gran, getting up from the couch. "I think you've been watching too much HBO, missy. Didn't I tell you never to watch HBO? Those shows will give you ideas."

"I only watch what you watch," said Harriet, resting her chin on her paws and staring melancholically at Dr. Packer, who'd finally reached the hospital vestibule and was now locked in a staring contest with the receptionist, a voluptuous blonde named Mandy.

Mandy and Dr. Packer had shared many intimate moments in the doctor's office, and as the camera zoomed in on a discarded pregnancy test in the reception wastepaper basket, Gran gasped. "She's pregnant! Mandy is going to have Dr. Packer's baby!"

"Darlene probably wants Brutus's babies," Harriet commented with a sigh. "Too bad he's been snipped. Maybe I should tell her. Maybe I should tell all of cat choir that Brutus is that way. At least they'll know what they're getting."

"Oh, honey, forget about Brutus," said Gran. "It's his loss and your gain if he's too busy chasing skirts to see that he's missing out on the best thing that ever happened to him."

Harriet gave her a sad smile. "Gee, thanks, Gran. Maybe you should tell that to Brutus. He doesn't seem to have gotten that particular memo."

Just then, the door swung open and a small procession entered: Odelia was the first, followed by Marge, and then three cats: Max, Dooley and... Brutus.

Instantly, Harriet's back went up and so did her tail, which was distended to a degree Gran had never seen before. She was also making hissing sounds at the back of her throat.

"Harriet!" said Marge. "What's gotten into you all of a sudden!"

"Get that cat out of here," said Harriet in clipped tones. "Before I do something stupid."

"Harriet, sweetums!" Brutus cried. "Nothing happened!"

"Get. That. Cat. Out. Of. Here!"

"Tootsie roll, please!"

Harriet suddenly streaked towards Brutus, who produced a loud squeak and then streaked off, his tail between his legs, Harriet screaming, "And don't come back!"

CHAPTER 13

*B*rutus was wandering the streets of Hampton Cove, feeling lost and alone. More than the fact of being chased from his own home by his former girlfriend, it was the knowledge that he had only himself to blame for his predicament that stung. If only he hadn't been so stupid to try his fatal charms on Darlene. But the temptation had been too sweet to resist. She'd immediately invited him into the bushes for some nookie. Not that he would ever have allowed things to go that far. In fact, just when Harriet had descended on the scene with Max and Dooley, he'd already been forming the words in his mind: I'm sorry, Darlene. But there's only one cat for me and that's Harriet, so this is where I leave you. The words simply hadn't rolled from his tongue yet, and then he'd been distracted by a flash that had momentarily blinded him, and then Harriet had appeared.

Still, if he hadn't gone into those bushes with Darlene, he wouldn't have been blinded by a flash, and it wouldn't have looked as if he was sniffing Darlene's butt.

He knew exactly how it looked and it was bad. Now Harriet would never forgive him, and he'd never be allowed to go home again and he'd be forced to roam these streets forever...

He'd arrived in one of those small alleys Hampton Cove was rife with, and gave the dumpster that was positioned near a store's back entrance a dubious glance. Would he really have to eat from these dumpsters from now on? No more bowls filled to the rim for him? No more cozy couch to curl up on, or warm body to cuddle?

He heaved a deep sigh and felt sorrier for himself than he'd felt in a long time.

"What are you doing here?" asked a voice that cut like a knife.

He recognized that singular voice. And when a familiar head popped out of the dumpster moments later, he actually felt happy. "Hey, Clarice," he said. "How are you?"

"Oh, it's you," said Clarice, and disappeared into the dumpster again, only to pop out once more seconds later. "You don't look so hot, Brutus. Are you sick and dying?"

"Well, I did almost die this afternoon," he admitted. "But Chase saved me. And then I was chased out of my own home by my own girlfriend, so I have seen better days."

Clarice hesitated, then finally said, "You look hungry. I'll share my food with you."

"Gee, thanks," he said, perking up. After that visit to Vena, he'd been looking forward to having a nice bite to eat. Harriet had put a stop to that. "What are you having?"

Clarice jumped out of the dumpster and gracefully landed on all fours. She was a feral cat, and looked as mangy and flea-ridden as any cat that lived on the street. She was also tough as nails, though, and she was Brutus's friend. "It's over there," she said, looking left and right as she led the way. "Best and most juicy piece of meat I've found in ages."

"Yummy," said Brutus, his stomach already grumbling. He

hadn't realized how hungry he was before Clarice's kind and generous offer.

"I was just looking through that dumpster for some seasoning," she explained. "Even free cats like me like a bit of seasoning to spice up their meals, you understand."

"Oh, I do understand," he said. "It's all in the seasoning."

With a flourish, she removed a piece of newspaper. "Ta-dah."

Before them lay a sad-looking rat, still intact, head, tail and all. Brutus retched.

Clarice licked her lips. "Seeing as you're going to need this more than me right now, I'm going to let you have the first bite. I don't do this for just anyone, so choose carefully." She then leaned in and whispered, "Go for the hindquarters. They're particularly succulent." Brutus retched again, audibly this time, and Clarice studied him with a slight grin. "I should have known. You city slickers don't know a good thing when you see it."

"I'm much obliged, Clarice," said Brutus, his stomach having gone from anticipatory rumbling to violent retching, "but I'm going to have to pass. I'm not as hungry as I thought I was." He backtracked towards the mouth of the alley.

"City slickers," Clarice grumbled, shaking her head. She then dug in, or at least Brutus thought she did. He couldn't watch, turning away at the last moment. The munching and tearing sounds were bad enough.

He practically ran from the alley and into the road. And he would have been crushed by an oncoming vehicle if a bystander hadn't had the presence of mind to snap him up at the last second and save him from being squashed like a bug.

The car's driver didn't even slow down, clearly heedless of the tragedy he or she had almost caused. Brutus caught a glimpse of a yellow parka as the car took the next turn, and then it was gone.

"You should watch where you go, buddy," said the Good Samaritan who'd saved his life. Then: "Brutus? Is that you?"

Only now did Brutus realize that it was none other than Odelia's dad Tex.

"What are you doing out here?" Tex asked, tucking Brutus into the crook of his arm, gently stroking his fur.

"I was lost but now I'm found," said Brutus, who was starting to think that the men in Odelia's family had a curious habit of saving his life today.

"I better take you home with me," said Tex. "Did you get that guy's license plate? I could have sworn he was aiming for you, buddy. Probably one of those maniacs. Some people just hate cats. Don't know why but they just do."

And while Tex prattled on, Brutus suddenly remembered what the ducks had said: the man in the yellow parka. The man who killed Dany Cooper!

And now had almost killed him...

CHAPTER 14

I was lying on my favorite spot on the couch while Odelia was getting ready upstairs. She was going out again, presumably to do a bit of sleuthing, in spite of her uncle's instructions that she shouldn't. Dooley was on the floor, licking his tail, and Harriet, who'd opted to spend the night at Odelia's and not next door, was moping on the windowsill, catching those last few rays of the day before the sun called it a night and went to bed.

We had yet to mention 'the incident' and though I was keen to do so, I'd refrained from broaching the subject until Harriet was good and ready. I'm not much of a psychologist but even I know that women, and definitely female felines, can't stay quiet for long, especially when it concerns such a life-altering drama as the breakup of a relationship.

Harriet had already been darting anxious glances in my and Dooley's direction but I'd ignored them all, pretending to doze off. The television was on, switched to Nickelodeon, where an episode of *PAW Patrol*, of all things, was playing. Normally I hate *PAW Patrol*. I mean, who wants to watch a kids show about talking dogs? But today I didn't mind one bit. Even though I'm not fond of dogs, I know for a fact that these dogs are all fictitious. Why else would they be so nice? Real dogs are never nice. They're all smelly, nasty and possessed by a distinct anti-cat bias. In other words, not my kind of pets.

Dooley, taking a break from licking his tail, now looked up at me. "Max?"

"Mh?" I said, still pretending to be dozing. I didn't have to work hard at it. I was, in fact, pretty beat, after the emotions of the day, and could have used a long nap.

"Why is it that dogs are always depicted as assisting the police in their investigations but cats never are? While it's obvious that we're better equipped to be police pets than dogs?"

"Beats me, buddy. I guess the dog lobby holds more sway in Hollywood than the cat lobby."

This seemed to surprise Dooley, judging from the way his eyes went wide. "The dog lobby," he said reverently.

"Yeah, dogs have powerful representation in Hollywood. Has to be. Why else do they get so many shows and movies made? While cats get few opportunities to shine, if any."

"You know what, Max? I think you're right."

"I know I'm right."

"Look at all those dog shows. *Lassie, Benji, PAW Patrol*. And hardly any shows about cats being man's best friend. Even Richard Gere had a dog movie. *Hitachi*."

"I think it was *Hachi*."

"Obviously dogs have infiltrated Hollywood, and pushed cats out of the picture."

"Even Disney is guilty in that department," I said, darting a quick glance at Harriet. She was still moping, but I could tell she was dying to have a little chat about the topic that was near to her heart—and it wasn't the underrepresentation of cats in the entertainment industry. "Name me a cat movie

Disney made that depicts cats in a favorable light. I doubt you'll find one."

"*That Darn Cat?*" Dooley suggested. "*The Aristocats?*"

"Made in the stone ages," I said. "Any more recent examples?"

Dooley thought hard, but couldn't come up with a single one. "I'm sorry, Max. I don't... Oh! *Cats & Dogs*. There were cats in that one, weren't there?"

"Not Disney. And the cats were the villains," I said. "Which is exactly what the dog lobby wants. No, face it, Dooley. Cats should probably create a lobby, like the dogs have, and march on Hollywood, demanding equal representation."

"We should have our own franchise," Dooley agreed. "Like *Beethoven*, but with cats."

"Or our own shows, like *Lassie*, but with cats."

"Or even books. Like *Old Yeller*, but with cats."

"Will you two shut up about Hollywood for a moment," Harriet suddenly burst out.

"Well, excuse us if we care about how underrepresented we are in Hollywood," I said, feigning indignation.

"What I don't get is how you can still hang out with Brutus after what he did to me," Harriet said. "I'm your oldest friend, Max—not Brutus. I even distinctly remember you once calling him a usurper and an intruder in your own home. And now you're taking his side against me? I expected more from you. And you, Dooley."

"Me?" asked Dooley, surprised. "What did I do?"

"You chose Brutus over your oldest, dearest friend. And it's something I will never forgive you for."

Dooley seemed flabbergasted. I wasn't. Harriet is prone to these spells of drama. It's all those daytime soap operas she watches with Gran. They have affected her usually sunny disposition and made her prone to extreme melodramatic outbursts such as this latest one.

"I'll have you know that I haven't taken Brutus's side," I said.

"Me neither," said Dooley. "I can't take sides when I care for both sides equally."

"Well put, Dooley," I said.

"Besides, what were we supposed to do? Let Brutus drown?"

This was news to Harriet, apparently, for she jerked her head up from contemplating the setting sun and gave us a penetrating look. "Drown? What are you talking about?"

"Brutus almost drowned today," I said. "If Chase hadn't been there to pull him out of the duck pond, he wouldn't be here."

"Well, he isn't here," Dooley pointed out.

"That's because Harriet chased him away," I said. "Poor cat. First he almost died trying to extract vital information from a duck, then he had to take a needle in the neck from Vena, and when he finally arrives in his own home, what does he get? A furious female lashing out and chasing him away. He's probably out there right now, sleeping with the rats and the other vermin, no choice but to live a life on the street, like a common reject."

Harriet seemed to waver, then her expression hardened. "If he almost died, that serves him right. He shouldn't have been mooning over Darlene's backside like that."

"For your information, he wasn't mooning over Darlene's backside any more than Darlene was mooning over his."

"Darlene was mooning over Brutus's backside a little, Max," Dooley said.

"Fine. I'll grant you that. She lured Brutus into this rendezvous, but the moment Brutus realized his mistake, he immediately set the record straight. 'Frankly,' he told

Darlene, 'there's only one cat for me and that's Harriet. So I'm very sorry but I can't do this.'"

"And immediately buried his nose in her butt," said Harriet scathingly.

"He did no such thing,"

"You can argue your point all night long, Max," said Harriet, "but I know what I saw, and what I saw was Brutus getting ready to get down and dirty with Darlene and I, for one, am not the kind of cat who will stand for such nonsense."

Just at that moment, Odelia arrived down the stairs, and Tex waltzed in through the sliding glass door that gives out onto the backyard. I should probably warn you that in this family, nobody ever knocks. People just come barging in whenever they please.

"Hey, Dad" Odelia said. "Brutus!" she added when she saw who Tex was carrying.

Brutus looked a little rattled, and perhaps the fact that Harriet already had her back up again had something to do with that.

"Look who I found roaming the streets like a critter," said Tex good-naturedly. "And almost being run over, too."

"I was almost run over by the killer of that Dany Cooper girl," said Brutus, keeping a close eye on Harriet, who seemed ready to pounce.

"Run over!" Odelia exclaimed.

"That's the second time I almost died today," Brutus said, still eyeing Harriet keenly.

If these words were designed to exact a certain effect on the errant feline they didn't miss it. Harriet's distended tail shrunk back to normal proportions. But then she growled, "I don't care how many times you almost get run over, you filthy love rat. I just hope next time someone finally succeeds."

And after these particularly harsh words, she padded off in the direction of the sliding door, and then out. Before making her grand exit, though, she glanced over her shoulder. "From now on you're all dead to me," she said, addressing me and Dooley. "Adieu." And then she was off.

CHAPTER 15

*a*mid all this cat drama, Odelia had only focused on one thing. She approached Brutus, who was still staring after Harriet. "Did you just say you were almost run over?"

Brutus nodded. "The same man who killed Dany Cooper. At least I think he was. He was wearing a yellow parka and a baseball cap and sunglasses."

Odelia looked at her father.

"I'm sorry," said Tex. "I didn't get a good look at the driver."

"What about the car? License plate number?"

Tex frowned. "Um…"

"Oh, Dad…"

"I'm a doctor, honey, not a detective. I don't routinely scan cars for license plates or makes and models." He held up a finger. "I do think it was a blue car, but don't hold me to that. It could have been a trick of the light."

"It was blue," Brutus acknowledged. "And one of those boxy cars that are so popular with the British royal family."

Odelia thought for a moment, then she and her father said in unison, "Range Rover."

She took out her phone and brought up a picture of a Range Rover. "Is this the car you saw, Brutus?"

Brutus glanced at the picture and nodded. "Yup. Like I said. The boxy car those British royals are always promoting on TV."

It was true. For some reason the British royal family were always driving Range Rovers, almost as if they were employed as that company's PR representatives.

"And was he actually targeting you, you think?" she asked next.

"I think so. At least, he seemed to swerve in my direction and tried to run me down. So if that's not intentional it was a very strange coincidence."

"He switched lanes just so he could run down Brutus," Tex confirmed. "It looked intentional to me."

"I don't get it," said Odelia. "First this man kills my understudy and now he tries to run over my cat? What's going on?"

"It could be a coincidence," said Tex. "Maybe this man simply doesn't like cats, so when he saw the opportunity to run one over, he took it."

"And it's possible there's more than one man in a yellow parka," Max offered.

Odelia chewed her bottom lip. Max was right. Then again, her gut told her this was no coincidence. That these two events, the murder of Dany Cooper, and Brutus's brush with vehicular catslaughter, were related. This man was after something. And it had something to do with her.

Dad put his hand on her shoulder. "Odelia, honey. You better be careful. I don't know what's going on, but something tells me this man may be targeting you."

She placed her hand on top of his and gave him a smile. "Don't worry, Dad. I'll be careful."

She took her purse from the kitchen counter and moved to the door.

"You're going out?" asked Dad.

"A meeting with the rest of the Bard in the Park crew. The director called it. We're going to sit down and try to process what happened this afternoon. Also, we need to decide whether to do the shows or simply cancel the entire project."

"They're not seriously thinking about going through with the performances, are they?" asked Dad incredulously.

"You know what they say, Dad. The show must go on. A lot of people put a lot of work into this project. It would be a pity to let them down. As Wolf sees it, we'll dedicate the performances to Dany's memory. I think she would have liked that."

"But there's a maniac out there, targeting members of your troupe. Not to mention... you."

"It's all right, dad. Chase will be there tonight. I'll be perfectly safe."

"I'm not so sure," said Dad hesitantly. It was obvious he wasn't too happy about letting his only child walk out of the house and into a potentially life-threatening situation.

"Chase is there," she repeated. "He already saved one life today. He's prepared to guard others with his own."

"It's true," Brutus said. "Chase saved my life tonight."

"That was a brave thing to do," said Dad with a nod.

Odelia gave her cats a finger wave. "You guys better stay here tonight. There's a cat killer on the loose, so no cat choir, all right?"

This didn't seem to sit well with her cat troupe, but they grudgingly agreed.

And then she was off.

*W*olf had set up shop in Whitmore Manor, a huge place that belonged to Marcia Graydon, patron of the arts and one of Wolf's mother's oldest and dearest friends. The sizable manor was located near the beach, just outside of town. Wolf was staying there, and so were other members of the crew. At least the ones that weren't locals, like Odelia.

Dany Cooper had been staying there as well.

When Odelia arrived, Chase's car was already parked in the driveway, so she eased her own, slightly more dilapidated truck, right next to his newer model.

She hadn't seen much of Chase today. Uncle Alec had kept him busy working the case all day, even though he'd rushed home for a quick shower and some fresh clothes after his close encounter with a duck pond earlier. She was looking forward to seeing him again, and hopefully gleaning some information about the case. Even though Alec had made her promise to butt out this time, she couldn't very well be expected to butt out completely. Not when this maniac was targeting not only her understudy but also her cats. Besides, as she'd told her uncle, her editor expected a full write-up, and so did the readers of the Gazette.

The cop standing at attention at the door indicated just how serious Uncle Alec took the threat. She nodded a greeting at the policewoman.

"Chase is already here," she said. "He's been asking about you."

It was a little odd to have to learn about Chase's where-abouts from a third party, but then that was what happened when a detective and a reporter moved in together: in the heat of the moment, their schedules didn't always overlap. At least tonight they would.

The meeting was being held in the manor's large and

opulently furnished dining room, where the crew took their meals when they weren't rehearsing, either on location in the park or in the small theater in the basement.

When Odelia strode in, the room was already packed to capacity, people talking in hushed tones. Obviously the death of Dany had made a huge impression. Suddenly Odelia wondered if her dad hadn't been right when he suggested the shows should be canceled. But that wasn't up to her. It was Wolf's decision to make—and the producers.

Wolf now clapped his hands and the room went quiet.

Odelia caught a glimpse of Chase in a corner, his notebook out, talking to a woman who looked like the spitting image of Odelia. Her second understudy, Odelia knew.

"I know we're all deeply impressed and shocked by what happened at the park today," Wolf said. "I just want you all to know that the local police have the matter well in hand. They're on top of this terrible tragedy and the police chief himself has promised me in no uncertain terms that the full weight of his department is brought to bear on this case. They will not rest before they have the vile killer of our dear and sweet Dany Cooper in custody. New York doesn't have capital punishment, as far as I know, which seems like a pity, under the circumstances." He now gestured to Chase. "I'm sure you've all had a chance to meet Detective Kingsley, who's in charge of the investigation."

Chase gave a nod of acknowledgment, and Odelia couldn't help but notice how the eyes of all the women in the room sparkled just that little bit brighter. She was sure his actions at the park today, where he'd repeated Colin Firth's lakeside performance in *Pride and Prejudice*, only with a live audience instead of a film crew, had something to do with that.

"Please give the detective your full cooperation. Hold nothing back. Even the most innocuous encounter or throw-away comment someone made may be the vital clue that will lead the police to the killer." He clapped his hands again. "Now, about the shows. I know you're all anxious to find out what Conway and I have decided." He looked defiant. "We are not going to let this monster stop us from putting on the best Bard in the Park edition this part of the country has ever witnessed. We're going through with the shows as scheduled and we're going to dedicate them to Dany's memory."

Murmurs of agreement echoed through the room. It was obvious the director had struck the right note.

Odelia just hoped it would also prove to be the right decision.

CHAPTER 16

*O*delia had sidled up to the director, the very flamboyant Wolf Langdon. They'd had a good meeting, and Wolf had been both dignified and defiant. It was obvious from the applause he received at the end of his address that his words carried the approval of all those present.

"Did you know Dany well?" Odelia asked Wolf while she took a sip from her root beer float. Even though there was ample opportunity to drown one's sorrows in alcoholic beverages, Odelia had opted to keep a clear head and pick a non-alcoholic alternative.

"Not really," said Wolf. "I know she was a dedicated actress who aspired one day to star on Broadway."

"You didn't hire her?"

"No, I didn't. I leave those decisions to Conway, my producing partner. He's been with me for years and years and years and I trust his judgment implicitly. I hire the key people—the stars—and leave the rest to Con. Some people may feel that a director should micro-manage but I'm not of that conviction. There's enough on my plate already, and

Con knows exactly what I want. Were you and Dany close?"

"Not really," Odelia admitted. She'd hardly spoken to the girl throughout the preparatory stages of the production. Then again, suddenly being thrown into this project had been so overwhelming there had hardly been time to get to know every team member.

"She was a very studious young woman," said Wolf. "Always to be found digging into her ebook reader. She was probably the only person in this production who could recite the verses of the bard backward and forward. She'd read all of his work and was a big fan." He smiled a wistful smile at the memory. "A dedicated little wench, our Dany Cooper."

"I find Shakespeare's words a little... opaque," Odelia said.

"I know. He's tough to wade through. There's an app I use. It adds little side notes and explanatory popups to put his words in the right historical context. Here. I'll show you."

He took out his smartphone and called up the app. And as it loaded, Odelia could see, in a flash, a message Dany had sent Wolf. It read: 'Hurry up, Wolfy. I'm naked and ready.'

It disappeared before she could read more, supplanted by the iconic face of William Shakespeare. And as Wolf went on to demonstrate the app, she wondered if she should say something. He made no indication to have noticed himself, though, and the moment passed.

So Wolf had known Dany a lot better than he admitted, huh? Weird...

Wolf was called away to deal with a creative dispute between two actors, and Odelia searched around for Chase, wondering where he'd gone off too. She saw he was chatting amicably with a pretty young actress. The woman had draped her hand on Chase's arm and was laughing just a little too loudly at a joke Chase was apparently telling her. A twinge of jealousy sliced through Odelia at the sight of her boyfriend chatting up another woman, and suddenly she could relate to Harriet's annoyance at seeing Brutus sniffing another cat's butt. Not that Chase was sniffing the woman's butt, but if left to his own devices he looked as if he were on the verge of doing just that.

She abruptly turned, and almost bumped into Don Stryker, who'd been standing right behind her.

"Oh, how the mighty have fallen," he said, steadying her by placing both hands on her upper arms. He immediately let go again, but not before giving her a gentle caress that sent shivers running down her spine—and not the good kind of shivers.

"What are you talking about?" she asked, quickly composing herself.

"The great and powerful Detective Kingsley. Obviously even our stalwart upholder of the law isn't immune to the charms of the innocent and beguiling ingénue."

"I don't know what you're talking about," she said, more brusquely than she intended.

He laughed an obnoxious laugh. "Oh, dear me. Hell hath no fury like a woman scorned. Detective Kingsley, if I'm not mistaken, is not getting any tonight."

"Oh, Don," she said. "You are—"

"Incorrigible? That, I am. And if you care to apply that age-old remedy for the wandering eye, my dear, I'm all yours." He gave her a wink. "Use me as you see fit."

Ugh. "No, thank you."

"Not that! You do have a dirty mind, young lady. No, I was thinking more along the lines of this scenario: you pretend to laugh uproariously when I whisper something in your ear, and I can promise you the handsome detective will suddenly find the company of the delectable Miss Grey a lot less appealing."

He'd taken her hand again, and she jerked it free. Having

to kiss this man was bad enough, but she drew the line at having to undergo his repulsive flirtations.

"Let's make one thing clear, Don," she said. "I am not now, have never been, nor will I ever be, interested in you, so bury those romantic notions or you'll be very disappointed."

"And already the lady starts to adopt the language of the bard," he said, and faux-applauded. "Bravo, Odelia Poole. Bravo, indeed."

"Oh, can it, buddy," she said.

"Not very Shakespearian, but I get your point," he said with a smirk. He glanced around. "What did you think of our great leader's speech? Not giving in to murderous bastards and all that?"

"I think he's right. We shouldn't stop this production just because of one madman."

"You do realize that there are ulterior motives at play here, right?"

Odelia studied her co-star. "What do you mean?"

"Wolf isn't doing this for poor little Dany's sake. He's sunk every last dime he owns into his production company. If these shows get canceled he'll be broke, and so will his producing partner."

"But I thought they were the most successful producers on Broadway?"

"Bullshit," spat Don. "Dear old Wolf has a serious gambling problem. When he's not studying the works of the bard, he can usually be found in Las Vegas squandering other people's money."

This was food for thought. "You don't think he had something to do with Dany's death, do you?"

Don gave her another one of his trademark smirks. "Very perceptive of you, my dear. Your reputation as Hampton Cove's premier sleuth precedes you. Yes, I do think he had something to do with Dany's murder and that's what I told that police detective of yours. Unfortunately he didn't seem to like the aspersions I cast upon divine Wolf's character."

"But why would he jeopardize his own production? Dany's death might have caused this whole thing to collapse, and then, as you said, he would have destroyed his own company."

"Oh, Odelia, Odelia," he said, shaking his head as if addressing a wayward child. "Don't you see? Dear Dany was blackmailing Wolf. The two of them were engaged in a torrid affair, behind Wolf's long-suffering wife's back, of course. If Wolf ended the affair, Dany threatened to spill the goods—talk to the enemy of every creative person in the world: the tabloids. And New York's tabloids can be notoriously vicious when they smell blood in the water. Already they were circling, and Dany's stories, whatever they were, could have seriously tarnished his reputation."

And with these ominous words, he left her to wonder about that message. 'Hurry up, Wolfy. I'm naked and ready.' It didn't sound like the message from a girl threatening blackmail.

CHAPTER 17

*C*onway Kemp was refilling his glass at the drinks table. Judging from the misty look in his eyes, it wasn't his first. Or his fifth. Odelia had seen him imbibe drink before, though, and therefore knew he could hold his liquor well.

"Hey, Con," she said, remembering their first meeting with fondness. In spite of Wolf's statement that he always hired the core crew himself, leaving only the bit players and the technical staff to Con's eagle-eyed judgment, he'd actually been the one to tap her for this role. She'd never had acting ambitions before, being content to be a small-town reporter and occasional sleuthhound, so when Con walked up to her three weeks ago in the local deli and asked her if she had any acting experience, she'd been highly surprised to say the least. Her answer had been a big laugh, which told him everything he needed to know.

"I've read your articles," he'd said, "and I've watched your YouTube channel. And I know this may come as a surprise to you, but have you ever considered acting?"

"Never," had been her instant reply, followed by more

laughter. Simply the idea of being an actress sounded ridiculous to her, and that's what she'd told Con.

A classically handsome man in his early forties, Conway Kemp had clearly been around the block a few times. Later she'd discovered, over a cup of coffee at Cup o' Mika, that he was an ex-marine, and that he'd only stumbled into the theater business by accident. His captain in the marines was Wolf Langdon's father, and he'd asked Con to keep an eye on Wolf when he first decided to enter the theater business as a young man. Con had quickly become responsible for Wolf's security, not a luxury as Wolf had initially made a name for himself setting up street theater productions in some of New York's roughest neighborhoods. Con had been his security detail, creative sounding board and assistant all rolled into one. Once Wolf had accepted an offer to direct his first Broadway play, Con figured his role was finished. Broadway might be tough to launch a career, but it was hardly the kind of place where you could get a knife planted in your back if you upset the wrong people.

But Wolf had made Con an offer he couldn't refuse: set up a production company together, financed by the woman Wolf would go on to marry, and after some hesitation Con had agreed. They'd quickly settled into their respective roles: Con took care of the business side, with Wolf handling the creative stuff. But part of Con's duties was also scouting new young talent to put in minor roles. This entailed trolling YouTube for fresh faces. Like Odelia.

"Hey, Odelia," he said now, slurring his words only a tiny bit.

"I can't imagine how tough this must be on you," she said. Con had been the one to recruit Dany, after all.

He nodded. "Yeah, it's the first time since I entered civilian life that I've lost a member of my team. Like you said, it's tough." He shook his head. "She was so young and full of life. A rising star. I'd already offered her a part in Wolf's next Broadway gig. She was going places, that kid."

"Do you have any clue who might have done this to her?"

"Not a one. I've been wracking my brain. Why kill the loveliest, most innocent and sweetest soul on the planet? I mean, if you're going to kill someone, why not kill that guy?"

Odelia followed his gesture, and saw he was directing a scathing look at Don Stryker. To be honest, she harbored some harsh thoughts about the man herself, but murder?

"I don't think we should say such things," she said therefore.

"No, of course," he said. "I'm sorry. It's just that... Of all people—why Dany?"

The fervor with which he spoke these words suddenly made Odelia suspect there was more than professional interest at play here. "You liked her, didn't you?" she said.

He nodded, staring down into his drink. "She was a lot of fun to be around."

"There's a rumor going around that... Wolf and Dany were an item."

Con didn't look up, nor did he respond.

"And that she was blackmailing him?" she prodded.

He looked up, and she was surprised at the anger that flashed in his eyes. "She was too good for a guy like Wolf. Too sweet and too innocent. If only I'd known..." He abruptly stopped himself when he realized who he was talking to, then plastered a tight smile on his face. "I'm sorry. I've had too much to drink, and I'm boring you with my sad sack stories."

"No, that's all right. Do you think Wolf could have some-thing to do with Dany's death?"

He stared at her for a moment, then abruptly turned away and left her standing there.

"Well, it's as good an answer as any, I guess," she muttered to herself. It told her that she should probably look deeper into this affair between Wolf and Dany. She suddenly caught sight of Wolf's assistant Kerry, who stood cuddling Wolf's beloved Chihuahua. A thought suddenly occurred to her, and a slow smile crept up her face.

Yes. This was exactly the kind of assignment Max and Dooley would love.

CHAPTER 18

A tense hush had descended upon the house. Dooley and I were keeping Brutus company, even though I really didn't want to choose sides on this one. Still, I could hardly leave the poor guy alone in this, his darkest hour. What I really wanted to do was attend cat choir and maybe sniff around the crime scene a bit more. You never know who else might have caught a glimpse of the killer. I mean, potentially a murder taking place in a park is seen by dozens of witnesses: the birds sitting in the tree overlooking the spot where the killer has chosen to plunge a knife into his hapless victim's chest, a dog sniffing that same tree and contemplating making a small deposit, even the earthworms popping up for a bit of fresh air, or the moles taking a break from digging their holes—though the latter have notoriously bad eyesight and might not be the most reliable witnesses imaginable.

And then there were the aforementioned ducks quietly quacking away in the pond. Brutus had persuaded one duck to come forward and volunteer a formal witness statement, but perhaps there were other ducks—the quiet ones who rarely quacked—who'd seen more and could provide the telling clue. The mole on the killer's nose. The harelip he carefully tried to hide beneath a bushy mustache. Or even the cleft chin that made him oh, so attractive to the opposite sex —a fact which will always puzzle me. Why are cleft chins so attractive to the human female? It's a chin. With a cleft. Nothing special.

So there really was a lot of work to be done, and all I could do was sit there and babysit Brutus and nurse his wounded soul. Such a shame.

"Did you see the look on her face?" he said. "It spoke volumes."

It did speak volumes. Volumes of verbal abuse. "It's all those soap operas," I repeated my favorite theory as to Harriet's terrible temper. "If only she would watch more of the always pleasant Hallmark Channel, she might not be this unreasonable all the time."

Brutus snapped his head up. "Harriet is not unreasonable. She's the most reasonable feline in existence. In fact she's put up with my horrible habits all this time, not a whisper of annoyance crossing her lips."

I'd heard plenty of whispers of annoyance pass Harriet's lips—in fact they weren't whispers but more fully formed sentences, very eloquently and colorfully expressed. I wasn't going to play devil's advocate right now, though, so I wisely shut up. If Brutus wanted to believe Harriet was an angel sent by the heavens to walk this sacred earth, so be it.

"She used to call me all these wonderful names. Tootsie roll. Snuggle bunny. Twinkle toes. Baby boo. And now all she can say is what a cad I've been—and she's right!" he wailed.

He was sitting slumped on the couch, his paws sticking out, his otherwise shiny black fur unkempt and looking dull in spots. In fact he looked like the epitome of the jilted male.

Which he was. Only he'd jilted her first, if we were going to split hairs.

"Did you know that the spiny dogfish shark's pregnancy lasts two years?" asked Dooley, who was watching the Discovery Channel, which was playing quietly in the background.

"No, I didn't know that," I said.

Silence reigned for a moment.

"Did you know unborn sharks sometimes eat their siblings?"

I groaned softly.

"And that sharks can have up to 35,000 teeth in their lifetime? Imagine being a shark dentist! Ha ha."

"Ha ha," I said without enthusiasm.

Once again, silence hung heavy in Odelia's small salon. Except for the shark show which apparently was on.

"Did you know—"

"Dooley! Enough with the sharks already!"

Silence returned, with Dooley looking offended.

"Max?" asked Brutus at length.

"Mh?"

"Could you give Harriet a message? I know she won't listen to me, but maybe she'll listen to you."

I was about to graciously say no to this idea when I figured that the sooner Harriet and Brutus reconciled, the sooner the four of us could be out there hunting for clues again.

"Fine," I said therefore. "What do you want me to tell her?"

"Tell her..." He frowned, then directed a curious glance at me. "What do you think I should tell her?"

"Oh, for Pete's sake," I exclaimed. "How should I know? She's your girlfriend!"

"Yes, but you've known her all her life. You know what might swing the deal."

I rolled my eyes. I'm not your poetic type, so I had no idea what to tell a jilted woman who's decided to jilt her boyfriend in return.

"Tell her you're slowly pining away in remorseful sorrow," suddenly Dooley said.

We both stared at him. It made for a nice change from the shark trivia.

"And tell her that soon there will be nothing left but a greasy spot on the couch."

Brutus pursed his lips. "I'm not sure I like it, but it is very powerful. Especially that part about the greasy spot. Max," he said, making a swift decision, "go for it, buddy."

"Oh, all right," I said, dragging myself up from my comfortable position on the couch.

I slouched to the kitchen door, shuffled through the pet flap, slumped through the backyard, wormed myself through the hole in the hedge, shambled through Marge and Tex's backyard, shoved myself through the second cat flap and crawled into the house and into the family room. No sign of sharks there. Instead, a rerun of *Scandal* was on, and the president was getting a tongue-lashing from his chief of staff. Uh-oh. This didn't bode well.

"Harriet," I said, arriving at the foot of the couch that held Gran, Marge, Tex and Harriet, all lined up like so many statues, eagerly following the exploits of *Scandal's* not-so-monogamous president.

"What do you want?" Harriet grunted.

"Message from Brutus," I said, hoping this would attract her attention.

"Whatever it is, I'm not interested," she said, making her meaning perfectly clear by flashing a shiny claw.

I gulped. I may have a layer of fat to protect me from claws like that, but I'm not immune to pain. In fact I hate it.

"Oh, just hear the cat out," said Gran.

"What is he saying?" asked Tex.

"He says he has a message from Brutus," said Marge.

"Let's hear it," said Gran. "And be quick about it. Something's about to happen with Twisty Fitzy and I don't want to miss it."

"We saw this episode already, Mom," said Marge.

"I know. But I've forgotten. And don't you remind me!"

"Brutus says he's in…" Dang. Now I couldn't remember what it was Brutus wanted me to say. So I decided to do what all good actors do: wing it!

"Well?" said Harriet, impatiently tapping that nail on the edge of the couch.

"Brutus says you're the love of his life and every second he can't spend with you is a second lost forever. He's in decline, losing weight so fast soon there'll be nothing left but a smudge on the couch." There. It wasn't verbatim, but I figured I'd gotten the gist of the thing nicely across.

Harriet appeared unmoved, however. "Tell him I don't care if he dies and rots in hell," she growled.

"Harriet," Marge said warningly. "Language."

"Oh, all right. Tell him I'll be happy to dance on his smudge."

"Harriet!" said Marge. "Brutus is still a member of this family and you'll treat him with respect."

"He doesn't respect me, so why should I respect him?" she challenged.

"Prima donna," Gran muttered.

"I heard that," Harriet snapped. "And I resent the slur."

"What is she talking about?" asked Tex.

"Nothing worth listening to," said Marge.

"Oh," said Tex, disappointed.

"Lovers' tiff," Gran clarified.

"This is not a lovers' tiff!" Harriet said. "He cheated on me and if I never set eyes on that black cat again, it'll be too soon! And you tell him I said that," she added for my sake.

So off I went again, this time in the opposite direction. Slouching, slumping, shuffling, worming and finally wending my way home. I arrived at the house, where I was met by two eager eyes boring into mine. Brutus was actually panting. "And? And? What did she say?"

I decided to keep this whole thing PC. "I think you're going to have to try harder, Brutus," I said. "She wasn't receptive to the whole concept of the, um, smudge-on-the-couch thing."

"What do you mean, she wasn't receptive?" asked Dooley. "That was some of my best work. Though it's a greasy spot, not a smudge."

"Hold your horses, Shakespeare," I said. "I think it's going to take more than a few well-wrought sentences to convince Harriet to clasp Brutus to her bosom once again."

"Oh, to be pressed to my love's bosom," said Brutus, suddenly becoming lyrical.

"You probably didn't do my words justice," said Dooley. "Next time I'll come with you." He shook his head. "If you want something done, you have to do it yourself."

"Next time?" I said. "There's not going to be a next time. You asked me to be your go-between and I was. Now I'm going to take a nap and try to forget this whole business."

"Wait!" Brutus said. "Please, Max. You have to help me. You're the only friend I've got."

"And what am I? Chopped liver?" asked Dooley. "I'm your friend, too, Brutus."

"Of course," said Brutus. "And I can't thank you enough. Now, please, tell Harriet... Oh, dammit! Why can't I think of the right words to say?"

Dooley touched his paw to his chest. "Allow *moi*, my friend. I'll give you all the words." He assumed the position of Rodin's The Thinker for a moment, then said, "Harriet, love of my life. Treasure of my heart. Please accept my deepest, most heartfelt apologies. I'm a swine, a creep, a louse. I'm less than the dirt under your nails, worse than the most disgusting rat that slinks through the sewers of this town, filthier than the creepy crawlies that slither from underneath an overturned rock. I'm filth, I'm slime, I'm nothing, I'm—"

"Yeah, yeah, yeah," Brutus grumbled. "I get the picture."

Dooley pointed an imperious finger in my direction. "Messenger. Deliver my decree."

"Oh, for crying out loud," I said. "You deliver your decree."

"Better yet, we'll deliver my decree together," Dooley said. Then, addressing Brutus, added, "Don't you worry about a thing. When in doubt, grovel, and I'm about to grovel on your behalf like no cat has ever groveled since that first cat crawled out of the woods and offered his services as a mouser to that first human in exchange for a roof over his head."

And off we went, with Brutus's halfhearted blessings, to heal this rift.

"Now what is it?" Harriet said, none too pleased with my swift return.

This time I was prepared to let Dooley do the talking. He didn't disappoint.

He knelt in front of Harriet. "Oh, great and noble one. Oh, most beautiful cat in all of existence. Oh, most gorgeous creature ever to walk the face of this earth. Oh, sweet and—"

"Yeah, yeah, yeah," she said. "Get on with it." She looked oddly pleased, though. Never underestimate the power of a compliment. Or a barrage of them.

"Brutus wants you to know he's deeply, sincerely sorry. He also wants you to know that he knows that you know that he's less than the dirt under your claws, less than the rats that infest the nooks and crannies of this town. Less than the muck that oozes out of the pipes when you unscrew that bulbous thingy underneath the sink to unclog the drain."

"Yuck," Gran muttered.

"I know all that," said Harriet. "Now tell me something I don't know."

"What are they talking about?" asked Tex.

"Oh, more stuff," said Marge vaguely. "Harriet, don't you think it's time you forgave that poor cat?"

"No, I don't," she said. "He cheated on me with Darlene and I'll never forget and I'll definitely never forgive."

"He says he never sniffed Darlene's butt," I said, feeling it was time to set the record straight.

"Oh, please. Tell him he's a liar. I saw him sniff her butt."

"He was trying to tell her he wasn't interested. That he only loves you."

"He had his nose up her butt!"

"That was just a matter of perceptive," said Dooley.

"Perspective," I corrected.

"What?!" cried Harriet.

"Perspective. Like when you think an object is far away while in fact it's right in front of you. Darlene's butt was here, while Brutus's nose was there, and never the twain met."

"Yeah, right." She rolled her eyes, not impressed.

"Oh, give the cat a break," Marge said. "He almost drowned today."

"And was almost run over," Tex added, happy that for once he could follow.

"Yeah, he almost died twice today," Marge said.

Judging from Harriet's expression, almost wasn't good enough. She'd only be happy if Brutus was run over not once but three times in a row by a succession of vehicles, until he actually was a smudge on the asphalt, and preferably she'd see Darlene suffer the same fate.

"Let's go, Dooley," I said finally. "This is no good. We're wasting our time here."

"But he loves you, Harriet," said Dooley. "Doesn't that mean anything?"

Harriet hesitated, but then her expression hardened. "No, it doesn't. He hurt me, Dooley, and I'll never be able to forgive him for that."

And Dooley and I were both making our way back to the other house when he said, "I didn't know love was so complicated, Max."

"Oh, it is, buddy."

"Good thing we never got involved in something like that."

"Yeah, good thing," I agreed.

"I just hope Odelia and Chase never get into that kind of trouble. If we can't even reconcile two cats, how are we ever going to reconcile two humans?"

"Odelia and Chase are never going to get into that kind of trouble," I said. "And you know why? Because Chase is smart. And so is Odelia. They're both smart. And in love."

We entered the house and I was surprised to find Odelia seated on the couch, absentmindedly stroking Brutus's fur. She looked distraught.

"Oh, no!" I cried. "You broke up with Chase!"

CHAPTER 19

Odelia stared at Max. "Why would I break up with Chase?"

"Um, no reason," he said, looking sheepish after his outburst.

"And where is Harriet?"

"Next door. She won't talk to me," said Brutus sadly. He then looked up at Max and Dooley, who both shook their heads.

Odelia decided to ignore her cats' odd behavior. "You guys. I need to ask you a huge favor."

"Anything," said Max instantly.

"As long as it doesn't involve groveling to Harriet," said Dooley. "Because that doesn't work. And believe me, we tried. Oh, boy, did we try."

"Right," said Odelia after a moment's hesitation. "The thing is, I think Dany and Wolf Langdon were having an affair." In a few words, she briefed her cat menagerie about the events that had transpired at the meeting.

"So you want us to break into the manor and take a peek at Wolf's phone?" asked Max.

"No, I'll take care of that part myself. What I want you to do is talk to Wolf's pet. If Wolf and Dany were having an affair that ended badly, he'll know about it."

"Oh, Wolf has a pet. How nice. What kind of cat is it?" asked Max.

"It's not a cat. It's a Chihuahua."

Her three cats were silent for a beat, then Max cried, "A dog?! You want us to talk to a dog?"

"Not just any dog. A Chihuahua. I've seen him. He's a very sweet and cute little fella. I'm sure you'll get along great."

"Chihuahuas are dogs, Odelia," Dooley pointed out. "And as a rule we're not all that fond of dogs."

"We got along fine with the French bulldog that belonged to the Kenspeckles, remember?" said Max.

"That was an exception to the rule," said Brutus. "Most dogs are terrible creatures."

"Not this sweet, precious Chihuahua," Odelia insisted. "He's just so cute and cuddly and he has the sweetest, kindest disposition. You'll see. You'll just love, love, love him."

All three cats stared at her. Then Max took a deep breath and asked, "You're not thinking about adopting a dog, are you, Odelia?"

"N-no," she said, but her hesitation gave her away. They all started howling again, so she held up her hands. "I have no concrete plans in that direction. Honest! But Chase likes dogs, and since he lives here now, it's only fair to assume that at some point he'll want to get a dog again. As long as he hadn't settled down, that was out of the question, but now…"

"Oh, God," said Max, breathing heavy. "Oh, my God."

"This is the end," said Dooley. "Finished. Kaput."

"I hate my life," said Brutus. "I just hate it."

"You guys. I'm not saying we're going to get a dog right now. At some point in the future, though, we might. Just might. Teensy, tiny chance." She didn't want to lie to them, even if they didn't like it. Chase loved dogs, though, and she did, too. Most people fell into one of two categories: they were either a cat person or a dog person. Odelia, in spite of the fact that she could communicate with cats, loved both. And she was fairly sure that her cats would love whatever dog would grace their home with his or her presence in the future, too.

"Dogs eat babies, you know," said Dooley. "They do. I saw it on the Discovery channel."

"You did not," said Max, then realized what Dooley was trying to accomplish, and quickly changed his tune. "It's true. Dooley is right. I saw it myself. Dogs are notorious baby eaters. Snack on babies all the time. They like babies even more than bones. Truth."

"Not funny, Dooley," said Odelia. "Now are you guys ready? Because as soon as that house is quiet I want to be ready to move. And in order to know when the coast is clear, we're going to have to go on a stakeout."

"Stakeout!" Max cried. "Yay!"

"What is a stakeout?" asked Dooley. "Does it involve steak?"

"No, it does not involve steak," said Odelia. "It involves us sitting and watching in a car and looking at Whitmore Manor until all the lights are out and it's time to make a move."

"Is Harriet coming, too?" asked Brutus.

"Of course!" said Odelia. "It wouldn't be a stakeout if the gang wasn't all there, right?"

Brutus nodded morosely. The prospect of Harriet joining them didn't seem to fill him with joy, as she'd expected it would. Then again, her cats were acting weird tonight.

"Max, you better go and fetch Harriet. Tell her to get ready," she said, then went up the stairs to change into something stakeouty.

Five minutes later, she was dressed in black from head to toe: black leggings, black sneakers, black sweater. And she was toying with a black balaclava she'd once picked up at a second-hand store when suddenly she sensed she was no longer alone. She turned. Chase was studying her from the doorway.

"Going on a stakeout?" he asked, an expression of amusement on his face.

"Um, no, of course not. I'm... taking the cats for a walk."

"Babe, I may not know a lot about cats but one thing I do know is that you don't take a cat for a walk."

"Most cats, no. But my cats are special."

"That, they are." He walked up to her and pinned her arms to her side until he'd grasped the balaclava she'd been holding behind her back. He held it up. "Most dog walkers or, if such a thing exists, cat walkers, don't wear a mask. You're going to break into Whitmore Manor, aren't you?"

She laughed what she hoped was a careless laugh. "Of course not! Are you crazy? Why would I go and do a silly thing like that?"

"Because you discovered that Wolf Langdon and Dany Cooper were having an affair and you're hoping to find out more by breaking into Langdon's room and digging through his phone."

She laughed again, with less conviction. "How—how did you know? About the affair, I mean?"

"I'm a detective, Odelia. It's my job to know stuff like that. And I had a long talk with Langdon's wife this afternoon, who told me all about the affair. She also mentioned she assumes Langdon and Dany had been sexting a lot, but every time she tried to get her hands on her husband's phone he made sure he had it on him. He even sleeps with that phone, keeping it tucked away underneath his pillow, his hand on top of it, just in case."

"That's very unhealthy. All that radiation."

"That's more urban legend than scientific fact, though, isn't it?"

"Still," she said, and swallowed. Gazing into Chase's eyes it wasn't hard to see why criminals would succumb under the pressure of his quiet determination and confess all.

"All right!" she finally cried, throwing up her hands. "I'm going to stake out Whitmore Manor and break in under the cover of darkness to check out the guy's phone. So are you going to tell me I can't go?"

"Of course not. I'm going to tell you I'm coming with you. And I hope you won't tell your uncle, because this operation will be one hundred percent unsanctioned and if we get caught you'll have a great front-page story but I'll probably get fired."

"I won't tell my uncle if you won't," she said with a low voice and a smile on her face.

He tilted up her chin, then pressed a warm kiss to her lips. "Hey, there, partner in crime," he murmured. "I missed you tonight."

"You did? It wasn't clear from the way you were chatting up that blonde."

"I wasn't chatting up that blonde. I was trying to extract information from her."

"Hard to know the difference."

"That's what makes police work so fascinating: nothing is what it seems."

She smiled. "Do you still prefer brunettes over blondes?"

"I prefer this brunette," he said, then deepened the kiss.

A soft cough sounded behind them. When they turned, she saw it was Max. He was staring at them with a horrified expression on his furry face. "We're ready when you are."

CHAPTER 20

"I'm only doing this for Odelia," Harriet said for the tenth time since we'd gotten into Chase's truck.

The four of us were in the backseat, with Chase at the wheel and Odelia riding shotgun.

"We know you're only doing this for Odelia," I said. "And I, for one, think it's very noble of you to put aside your differences and join us."

"I haven't put aside any differences," said Harriet through gritted teeth. The words came out in a low growl and Chase frowned and checked his rearview mirror.

"One of your cats doesn't sound happy, babe," he said.

"Oh, she's probably nervous, that's all," said Odelia.

"Nervous? How can she be nervous? She doesn't have a clue where we're going."

"Cats have an instinct for these things," she explained.

"Um, I guess," he said doubtfully. Chase was not a big believer in the abilities of cats to solve murders. Then again, he also had no idea Odelia could understand every word we said and vice versa. Probably best to keep it that way, too, or else he might start interfering in this holy alliance between man and beast, as Tex had once called it.

"The only reason I'm going along on this trip is because Odelia asked me to," Harriet repeated, in case we hadn't heard her the first dozen times. "You're not off the hook, Brutus."

"I understand that and I regret it deeply," said Brutus. "What more can I do than to apologize once again for any misunderstanding my behavior may have caused and to—"

"Misunderstanding? That was no misunderstanding. Your nose was practically glued to Darlene's butt."

"It was a case of wrong perspective!" he cried.

"Yeah, just keep telling yourself that," she said, and looked out the window, determined not to give Brutus another glance.

"So what is our mission, Max?" asked Dooley.

"Mission. Nice," said Brutus with a chuckle. When Harriet shot him a frosty glance, breaking her own rule not to look at him, the chuckle turned into a choked chortle, then quickly died away.

"Our mission—should we choose to accept it—is to talk to that Chihuahua and extract information from the mutt with any means at our disposal."

"Chihuahua?" said Harriet, looking up in surprise. "Nobody said anything about a dog."

"A Chihuahua, as Odelia has gone to great pains to explain, is not just any dog. A Chihuahua is a noble breed and amongst the sweetest and most innocuous of its kind. I'm sure we'll get along great with the little mutt."

"I'm not going near that dog. No way. Dogs stink."

In the front seat, Odelia suppressed a snicker, causing Chase to give her a look of concern.

"Dogs don't stink," I said, with a glance at the back of Odelia's head. I was nothing if not a loyal soldier to my general. So I dutifully conveyed her words to the rest of her troops. "A dog may have a very particular odor, but to characterize that odor as foul is in the eye of the beholder."

"The nose of the beholder, you mean," said Harriet.

"Right."

"Dogs stink and I'm not coming near that mutt," she insisted. "And that's my final word. If you want to talk to the filthy creature, that's up to you. But I'm going to look for a more palatable and civilized creature to talk to. Every mansion worth its salt must have a cat roaming around someplace, and I'm going to find it."

"You just don't want to be near me. Admit it," said Brutus with a pained expression.

"I'm not admitting a thing until you admit your nose was so far up Darlene's butt you could fondle her tonsils."

"I'm not admitting something that didn't happen," said Brutus.

"Oh, you are going to confess, buster."

"This isn't a Syrian torture chamber and you can't make me confess a thing."

"Confess!" she screamed and flew across Dooley and my laps to tear into Brutus.

It took Odelia a little time to part both cats, and when finally she managed, Brutus had a bloody scratch across his nose and there was a drop of blood on Harriet's otherwise pristine white fur that hadn't been there before.

"And now behave, the both of you," said Odelia in a voice I hadn't heard her use before. She would have made a great taskmaster, I thought. Or owner of a kennel.

"You scratched me!" Brutus cried, aghast. "You actually drew blood!"

"Serves you right," said Harriet from her corner.

"My nose! It will never look the same again!"

"Show it to Darlene. Maybe she'll lick it for you."

"I'll have a scar!"

"I'm sure Darlene loves her men scarred."

"I don't care about Darlene!"

Dooley and I shared a look of concern. This cold war had just escalated into a full-blown hot war, and I wasn't sure I liked it. Once the gloves came off, there was no telling whose face Harriet would dig her claws into next. Already she'd determined Dooley and I were collaborating with the enemy, so all bets were off. From now on, no one was safe.

"So how are we going to sneak into the manor?" asked Chase.

"I thought you might have a plan. You're a cop, after all. Don't you cops get trained to pick locks and stuff?"

"We do, but since this was your idea I figured you had a plan all cooked up and ready to execute."

Brutus winced at the mention of the word execute. He darted a quick glance at Harriet, then continued licking his injured nose. For what it was worth, I figured it was only a small price to pay for his stupidity. Everyone in cat choir knew Darlene was a tease and a loose cat and everyone steered clear of her because of that fact. Now Brutus knew, too.

"I figured I'd just... wing it, you know," said Odelia.

Chase laughed. "Wing it. I like that. Why don't we simply go in through the basement? When I was checking out the manor this afternoon I noticed the lock is broken on the second basement window from the right. A good shove and we're in."

Odelia turned to Chase, a look of surprise on her face. "You were planning this before I even got the idea!"

"I wasn't planning anything. Just happened to check the perimeter for possible weaknesses and just happened to notice the window." His grin vanished. "Truth be told, Wolf asked us to give his security team a thorough screening.

Dany being killed in broad daylight like that? There is obviously something wrong with the way security is organized."

"I don't think Wolf has any security to speak of. At least not that I ever noticed."

"He has a few people on his payroll, but they're not highly skilled or organized. I told him to hire a professional crew and that's what he promised me he'd do."

"You also told him about the wonky window?"

The grin returned. "I decided to wait until after the new team arrived." He shrugged. "What? I know how your mind works, babe. You just love this breaking and entering stuff."

"I do love this breaking and entering stuff," she admitted. "And you know what else I love right now?"

"I have no idea," he said, his grin widening.

"You, you big doofus. C'mere."

"Not while I'm driving, babe."

"C'mere!"

There ensued yet another one of those scenes that are incredibly awkward for cats to watch.

Humans kissing.

Yuck.

CHAPTER 21

*I*t was well past midnight now, but the light in some of the windows of Whitmore Manor was still shining as bright as day. Then again, these were creative people. Actors. And clearly actors, like vampires, preferred to live at night and eschew daylight.

"Looks like they're not asleep yet," said Chase, glancing up at the three or four lit up windows. He settled back in his car seat, which he'd cranked back. "We're in for a long wait, babe."

"I'm going to let the cats out," she said. "They're not going to be comfortable cooped up inside the car. And she opened the door to let us out. We jumped at the chance. Well, all of us except Harriet, who still didn't seem keen to join in the nocturnal adventure.

I gave Odelia a wave of the tail goodbye and she closed the door again. I just knew there would be plenty more nookie and I was glad she'd spared us having to witness it.

"So how are we going to get in?" asked Brutus.

"You heard Chase. There's a wonky window near the back," I said. "I'm sure we'll be able to sneak in that way."

Chase had parked his car inside the Whitmore Manor domain. Clearly security left something to be desired, judging from the front gate which had been left wide open, and not a single guard placed at the entrance to halt our access to the manor. He'd parked under a big oak tree, to provide himself some measure of cover, and for them the long wait began. For us, the long trek through the manor began, in search of this illustrious Chihuahua.

Dooley and I quickly moved ahead, Harriet and Brutus trailing behind. At a certain point I heard Brutus exclaim, "It was a matter of perspective!" and I shook my head.

"Brutus really is in the doghouse, isn't he?" Dooley said.

"Or the cathouse, depending on your perspective," I said, and we both giggled like two silly kittens. Even though Brutus and Harriet might take this thing bloody seriously—literally—that didn't mean Dooley and I couldn't extract some merriment from the episode.

We found the window just where Chase had said it was, and snuck into the manor through the crack—dropping gracefully to the cement floor below. It was pretty dusty and dank-smelling in the basement, but then basements usually are.

Odelia had told me Langdon's bedroom was on the third floor, the last room on the left, so that was our destination. We snuck through the basement, which was just a collection of old furniture covered in white sheets gathering dust, snuck up the stairs, through a long corridor, and up more stairs, these ones marble instead of rickety wood.

Upstairs, we heard laughter and singing coming from one of the rooms, and I quickly snuck a peek. Four or five people were smoking something that had an acrid tinge to it that wasn't tobacco, and drinking a substance that wasn't lemonade. They looked as if they were having a whale of a time. They were also partly naked, so I quickly retreated. I'd been forced to witness enough human nookie for one day thank you very much.

The third floor proved more quiet and peaceful than the second, which was a good sign.

"I'm not sure about this, Max," Dooley said as we tiptoed underneath the portrait of a dour-looking man dressed in a hunter's outfit. Dogs were converging on a deer, and I felt for the poor deer.

"I'm not too sure about this either," I admitted. It was all well and good to describe this Chihuahua as a sweetheart and a cutie pie, but dogs are a treacherous breed. They can be sweet and cute one minute, then viciously turn on you the next. I was going to keep my options open and make sure I had my route of escape mapped out just in case.

"Do you think Brutus and Harriet got lost?" he asked as we paused to listen for sounds of human activity.

I glanced back to the stairs. There was no sign of either one of our two friends.

"I just hope they haven't killed each other," I said with a twinge of concern. That slash across the nose was still fresh in my mind, and the thought rankled.

"Maybe we should turn back," said Dooley, glancing up at yet another hunting print, this one depicting a brace of dogs tearing into a poor rabbit. It was definitely a bad omen.

"We need to press on," I told Dooley. "Odelia expects us to talk to this dog, so we need to talk to this dog."

We moved along the corridor, which was all dark paneled walls and oak parquet covered with a long and high-pile runner our paws sank into. The smell was musty, either from the smokers on the second floor, or the natural smell of an old manor.

We finally arrived at the last door on the left, and to my relief it was ajar. Cats, as you may or may not know, have a hard time opening doors. At least when they operate on a knob principle. Tough to turn a knob when all you have are soft pink pads, fur and claws.

We snuck into the room, careful not to make a sound. From inside, snoring drifted our way. And as we moved deeper into the room, a peaceful scene greeted us: there, in the middle of the room, a man was sleeping in a big four-poster bed, a dog draped across his feet. A night light had been left on, bathing the Hallmark-type scene in a soft golden hue.

"Aww," I said.

"How sweet," Dooley echoed.

At this, the doggie pricked up its ears, then sniffed the air, and finally spotted us.

He made a soft gulping sound, then abruptly jumped down from the bed and scooted behind the nightstand.

So much for the rabid, cat-devouring monster we'd been dreading to encounter.

CHAPTER 22

*O*delia was getting tired of sitting in a car waiting for a bunch of party people to finally go to bed. Not that she minded being cooped up in a small space with Chase —far from it—but she had another big day tomorrow, and she was one of those people who, when they didn't get enough sleep, were complete and utter wrecks the next day.

"When are they finally going to bed?" she grumbled, when she saw that in one room the lights were still on. "Don't they need to sleep?"

"They're young. They're free. And they probably want to get through the bag of weed Wolf provided—or maybe it was Conway Kemp. The stories tend to differ depending on the source."

"Weed? And you approve of this?

"Hey, as long as the politicians don't make up their minds, I'm not touching that."

"Is that what you and Miss Blonde talked about?"

"She did ask about the laws in the state of New York regarding the recreational use of marihuana," he said with a grin.

"And what did you tell her?"

"That marijuana is still illegal except for medical use on a strictly regulated basis. But that you won't get arrested for smoking in public unless you're driving a car or have a criminal record—at most you can expect a fine these days."

"Which you're not going to give them."

He shrugged. "I've got my orders, babe. Stuff is above my pay grade."

"Sounds like a pretty lame excuse to me."

He laughed. "I take it you're not a big fan of weed."

No, she wasn't, but that was not an argument she was prepared to get into right now. "What else did you talk about?"

"Well, about the affair Wolf and Dany were reportedly having."

"Nothing reportedly about it. Looks like everyone knew about it, except me."

"And Wolf's wife. Until not so long ago she was in the dark, too."

"So where is Mrs. Langdon?"

"Staying in town at the Star."

The Hampton Cove Star was a boutique hotel located right on Main Street. "The Star? Why not at the manor?"

"She was at the manor at first, but my guess is that she got tired of having to watch her husband getting frisky with Dany so she relocated to the Star."

"Have you talked to her?"

"Yes, as a matter of fact I have."

"Oh, someone's been a busy boy."

"Your uncle did urge us to handle this murder business quickly and with the utmost expedience so that's what I'm doing."

"And? What did Mrs. Langdon have to say?"

"She didn't exactly burst into tears when I told her about what happened to Dany."

"Which is understandable."

"Exactly. She admitted she'd heard the rumors, too, and that's why she moved to the Star. She also said she was considering divorcing Wolf, and she happened to mention that Wolf was not in a situation where he could afford a divorce. It's my understanding Mrs. Langdon is the source of much of Wolf's wealth. Her family is extremely well-off. He isn't."

"Do you think she might be responsible for Dany's death?"

"Nuh-uh. She was having lunch with a friend when Dany was killed. About a dozen guests and waitstaff can attest to that."

"Too bad. She would have been the perfect killer."

"Looks like we're up," said Chase, gesturing to the window where now the light had finally been extinguished.

"Finally. I thought they'd never go to bed."

They got out of the car and moved stealthily towards the manor, hunched over and staying in the shadows. There was a full moon out, so they'd have to be careful not to be seen.

They arrived at the back of the house and quickly snuck inside. Odelia hoped her cats had already had a chance to talk to Wolf's Chihuahua. If not, no harm done. They would get the necessary information some other way.

"There's one thing I don't get," she whispered as they snuck up a rickety staircase, and she flicked at what she hoped was a cobweb and not a hairy rat or other animal.

"What's that?" Chase whispered back.

"Can't you cops access phone records and stuff like that?"

"We can, but it takes time. And besides, it's a lot more fun sneaking around with you!"

She grinned. "You know what? This is actually the first

time you've joined me in this part of an investigation."

"True," he said. "And look how much fun we're having!"

Until then, Odelia had joined Chase for his police interviews from time to time, but he'd never joined her on her more improvised investigative outings. One technique she hadn't introduced him to was the part played by her cats. Maybe she'd never tell him about that. He might not take it well.

They'd arrived on the second landing and were now sneaking towards Wolf's room. She just hoped no one got it into their mind to open a door and bump into them. And just as she was thinking it, a door to their right opened and Don Stryker walked out and bumped straight into them!

He stared at her, his hair mussed up and sleep wrinkles all over his face.

Both Odelia and Chase stood frozen at the spot. Now they were in a real jam!

"Mom?" Don finally muttered. "Is that you?"

And then Odelia smelled it: the guy was totally baked!

"Yes, it's me," she said. "Now go back to sleep… Donny."

"Okay, Mom." He touched a finger to her cheek. "You look so young." He smiled a weak smile, blinked slowly, then staggered back into his room, closing the door behind him.

"See?" said Chase. "Weed is good!"

"Yeah, right," she said, and then they were hurrying towards the last door on the left. To her elation, it was ajar. And just as they entered, two cats came trotting out. Max and Dooley.

Max said, "The phone is on the nightstand," and she gave him a wink before he and Dooley disappeared down the hallway.

She briefly wondered what had happened to Harriet and Brutus, then shrugged off the thought and followed Chase into Wolf's bedroom.

CHAPTER 23

"I told you I'm not talking to that dog and I'm not talking to that dog!" Harriet was saying. In fact she'd rather be anywhere but there, but duty had called and Harriet wasn't one to shirk her duties. Once on the scene, though, she'd had one of her typical change of hearts. The prospect of sitting in a crowded room and chatting with some obnoxious odoriferous canine was too much for her, and she decided to turn back and go and sit in the car. Odelia would understand, she knew. She would give her a cuddle and that would be it.

Today had already been a day of high emotion and the dog thing simply was too much! No dogs! Not on top of everything else that had happened!

Brutus, of course, didn't understand. That was a dude for you.

"But we have to talk to the dog!" he said. "We promised!"

"No, Brutus. I'm not doing it. If you want to talk to the dog, go right ahead and do it. But I'm not going anywhere near that smelly mutt."

"Oh, you don't know if he's smelly. Maybe he smells like a

rose. I've met dogs that smelled to lavender, expensive French perfume, even licorice! Humans are crazy that way."

She knew humans were crazy. She'd lived with them long enough. But not as crazy as Brutus, for throwing away the love they shared for a chance to sniff some skank's butt.

"I want to be alone now, Brutus," she said as dignified as she could.

But of course he wouldn't listen. "I'm telling you, it's a matter of perspective. My nose was nowhere near Darlene's butt. It only looked that way from where you were standing."

"You were there. Darlene was there. Enough said. Now please leave me alone."

"I know it was a mistake for me to follow her there. I admit that," he said, tapping his chest. "But the moment I realized my mistake, I told her! Or at least I was going to tell her."

"You were going to tell her with your nose buried up her butt? Nice try, Brutus. I'm not buying it. Now go away."

"It's a matter of perspective!"

"Oh, buzz off, buster," she said, and stalked off. This time, at least he had the decency not to follow her.

She hadn't lied. She did want to be alone. She'd been with Brutus for so long now it was hard to imagine her life without him. She truly loved the butch cat, from the moment he'd come into her life, all bluster and big talk. She'd seen right through that, of course. She'd known instinctively that underneath all that bluster lurked a tender soul and a good heart.

She also knew that he probably realized he'd made a mistake by following Darlene into that clearing—or had she followed him? It was hard to say, and she wasn't going to take either Darlene or Brutus's word for it. They were both lying through their teeth, both for different reasons. But she found it hard to forgive him. If a tomcat strays once, he'll stray again. It's just the way they're built. Max, she knew, would never stray once he gave his heart to a cat. And nor would Dooley. Until now she'd believed Brutus wouldn't either.

That's why the whole thing with Darlene had shocked her to the core. And now she didn't know what to believe. All she knew was that she didn't want to see Brutus. At least not for a while. Until she decided how to proceed.

🐾

*B*rutus walked off, and kicked a rock as he did. This was probably the worst day of his life. Or at least up there among them. It reminded him of the day Chase's mother had decided to hand him off to her son. Chase's mom hadn't been well, and decided she couldn't be trusted to take care of her cat. Besides, she was moving in with her sister, who wasn't allowed to keep pets in her rent-controlled Bronx apartment. So on to Chase he went, and then lady luck had come through for him and he'd found a new home. Even better than before: a home with great humans, and three great cats who he now considered family.

It had been tough in the beginning, though. He and Max had clashed frequently. He'd had the mistaken belief at the time that only one cat could rule the home and he'd decided that he was that cat. Now he realized there didn't have to be one cat in charge. They were all in charge. Max had opened his eyes to that, as had Dooley. And Harriet, of course.

Brutus had never known love before. Now he did. And then he'd gone and lost it.

He was such a moron, wasn't he? And he was just kicking another rock when suddenly the ground opened up underneath him and he was falling. Fully expecting to fall into some abyss or ravine, he let out a squeal. Suddenly his fall was broken by a soft object.

"Hey, little buddy," the soft object spoke, and looking up Brutus realized he'd been caught by a friendly giant.

Looking up even further, he saw he'd dropped off a cliff. A sort of man-made promontory that overlooked another duck pond. And by the side of that pond, a man had been sleeping off his hangover—at least judging from the powerful smell of booze on him.

Dang it! This was the third time he'd almost died today!

CHAPTER 24

$\mathcal{D}$ooley and I snuck further into the room, adamant to talk to that dog, whether he liked it or not. And obviously he didn't like it one bit.

"Hey, dog," I said, in a bid to get him to come from behind the nightstand. "Nice doggie, doggie."

"We just want to talk to you," said Dooley.

In the bed just by our side, Wolf Langdon stirred. No matter how softly we talked, our meowing probably disturbed his slumber. We needed to do this fast, before he woke up and kicked us out of his room!

"Doggie!" I loud-whispered. "We need to ask you a few questions."

"Yeah, it's not as if we're going to bite you or something," Dooley chimed in.

We both laughed at that. Just the idea. Cats biting a dog! Ha ha.

But the Chihuahua didn't laugh along. He probably wasn't in on the joke.

"Look, we're cat detectives," I said, "And we're trying to figure out who killed Dany Cooper."

"Do you know who Dany Cooper was?" asked Dooley.

"I know who Dany was," the dog said, in a scared little voice. He didn't sound or behave like any dog I'd ever met.

"Well, she was murdered this afternoon," I said, "so we're trying to figure out who did it."

"You're not going to hurt me?" asked the doggie.

"Of course not. Why would we want to hurt you?" I said, more abruptly than I intended.

"Oh, please don't scratch me," said the doggie. "A cat once scratched me and I didn't like it."

"We're not the scratching kind," I assured him.

"I'm sure glad Harriet didn't come along," Dooley whispered. "She would have scratched him for sure."

"Dooley, shush," I said. Addressing the Chihuahua, I repeated, "We don't scratch dogs, dog. Usually it's the other way around."

"Yeah, dogs like to bite us, for some reason," Dooley added. "No idea why. We're not that tasty, as far as I know."

"I'm not going to bite you," said the doggie. "I never bite anyone—except my bone, of course. I like to chew my bone."

"Well, that's all right," I said. "You won't bite us and we won't scratch you. Deal?"

"Um, okay," he said, then reluctantly came crawling out from behind the nightstand.

He looked funny, with his big ears and his short body. His tail was down and he still looked pretty scared.

It was a novel experience. No dog had ever been afraid of me before.

"So what do you know about Dany Cooper?" I asked.

"She was nice. And my master liked her a lot. And I do mean a lot."

"How do you know?"

"Well, they were putting their lips together a lot, and they spent an awful lot of time naked in bed together."

Dooley and I were silent for a beat, then Dooley said, "Yeah, I guess they did like each other a lot."

"Do you think your master could have something to do with Dany's death?"

"Like what?"

"Like maybe he killed her?"

The dog cocked his head and stared at me. "I don't get it."

He didn't strike me as the sharpest dog in the shed, so I repeated the question. "Did Wolf kill Dany?"

"But why would he kill her? He kept telling her he loved her. He'd also bought her a big ring and he said he was going to marry her as soon as his wife signed off on the divorce."

"Divorce? Wolf was getting a divorce?"

"Sure. At least that's what he told Dany. I don't think he told Emily, though."

"Emily?"

"Wolf's wife. She's very sweet. She was here, and then she wasn't. I don't think she liked it that Wolf spent so much time with Dany, even though he said he didn't." He shook his little head. "Humans are weird."

"Tell me about it," I said with a sigh.

"Anyway, Wolf loved Dany, so he would never hurt her. Besides, I was sitting next to him the whole time, so if he had killed her, don't you think I would have noticed?"

So there went that particular theory. "I guess so."

"This is just so sad. Dany always gave me lots of cuddles and kisses. I liked her."

I suppressed a shiver. Who would want to kiss and cuddle a dog? Now that I was this close to him, I discovered Harriet was right. Dogs did smell. Some type of musky odor. Yuck.

"So exactly where were you when Dany was killed?" I heard Dooley ask. I was already moving back to the door, writing the interview off as a huge waste of time.

"I was right there. I actually saw her getting killed."

"Wait, what?" I said, turning back.

"Yeah, it wasn't pleasant," said the dog. "This human stood chatting with her, then suddenly they made a move and her face went all weird, and then she dropped down."

"Doggie," I said intently.

"You don't have to keep calling me doggie," said the doggie. "I have a name, you know, and it's Ringo."

"Ringo. Listen to me. This is very important. Who was that person?"

"I don't know. I think it was a man, judging from his posture, though I can't be sure. He had his back turned to me so I couldn't see his face. All I know is that he was wearing—"

"A yellow parka. Yeah, we know."

"If you knew already, why do you ask?" he said indignantly.

So maybe dogs are not so dumb after all.

"You never saw his face?" I asked, just to make sure.

"No, I didn't. But I can tell you who did. Mr. Owl."

"Mr. Owl," I said dubiously.

"Yeah. He always sits in that tree. I've seen him every time. He's very friendly, too. Always greets me with a nod and a kind word. He was in that tree today, so he must have seen the whole thing. You talk to Mr. Owl and he'll tell you who killed Dany."

I held out my paw and Ringo winced, probably expecting me to scratch him. Instead, I patted him on the shoulder. "Ringo. You have given us a vital clue."

"I have?" he said.

"You sure have. You may even have solved Dany's murder."

A smile slowly crept up Ringo's narrow face, and his big ears distended even wider, giving him an owlish look. "I like that," he said. "It's not nice when people kill other people, especially when they're sweet and kind, like Dany Cooper."

"You're absolutely right. And we're going to make sure the killer won't get away with it."

"Our human's boyfriend is a cop," Dooley explained. "So we tell our human who the killer is, and Chase makes sure he goes to prison."

"Wait, you can talk to your human? And they understand what you're saying?"

"She does. She's one of those rare humans who understand cat language."

Ringo cast a hopeful look at his inert human. "Boy, oh, boy. How I wish Wolf could understand me. The stories I would tell him!"

We said our goodbyes, and just as we left the room, Odelia and Chase entered. From behind us, Ringo asked, "And who are these people? Should I bark? Alert my master?"

"No, Ringo," I said. "These are the humans I was talking about. They're looking for your master's phone."

"On the nightstand. See ya, guys."

"See ya, buddy." To Odelia, as she entered, I said, "the phone is on the nightstand." She gave me a wink in return.

"I have to say, Max," said Dooley as we descended the stairs. "I may just have had a change of heart about dogs. They may not be as horrible and nasty as I always thought."

"We met nice dogs before, remember?"

"Yeah, but I always figured they were the exception that proved the rule. Now I'm not so sure."

"I'm not so sure either."

"When Odelia gets a dog, I sure hope it's a nice one like Ringo."

And I sure hoped she wouldn't get a dog. Nice or not, frankly speaking I was having enough trouble navigating the complicated relationships in Odelia's menagerie as it was.

CHAPTER 25

*O*delia snuck over to the nightstand, and grabbed Wolf's phone. So the stories of the director sleeping with his phone under his pillow were greatly exaggerated.

"Hello, little one," she whispered as she turned over the phone in her hand.

Next to her, Wolf stirred in his sleep, muttered something, then turned to his other side and went right back to snoring softly.

Meanwhile, the Chihuahua sat studying her every move. He'd clearly been briefed by Max, or else he would have barked his little head off.

She tiptoed back to where Chase was checking the pockets of Wolf's jacket and together they clicked the phone to life. The screen lock was one of those password patterns.

She glanced at the doggie, which sat staring at her unblinkingly. Too bad she didn't speak a dog's language. And too bad Max and Dooley had already left, for they could talk to any animal in existence, apparently, and then relate what they told them to her. Her finger hovered over the phone, but Chase shook his head.

"Three attempts and the phone will be locked. Better not risk it."

They hadn't really thought this through, had they?

Just then, the little doggie softly barked once.

She turned to him and saw he was still eyeing her intently. He then did the most amazing thing. He slashed the air like Zorro used to do with his sword, creating the letter Z.

Both Chase and Odelia stared at the dog, who seemed to roll his eyes, then repeated the gesture. Slash. Yep. Just like Zorro.

She glanced down at the phone in her hand. Could it be?

Chase shook his head and mouthed, 'No! Don't do it!'

She decided to throw caution to the wind and traced the letter Z across the small panel, connecting the dots. Instantly the phone unlocked and she made a little fist pump.

'Omigod,' Chase mouthed. He couldn't believe it either.

Odelia turned to the Chihuahua and nodded her thanks. And she could have sworn the dog actually smiled!

She immediately called up the email app and scrolled through Wolf's emails. When she saw he had a hundred unread ones, she typed Dany into the search window. Nothing. She thought for a moment, then brought up the WhatsApp app. And immediately hit the motherlode. She scrolled through Dany and Wolf's chats. It was all pretty saucy stuff.

"Mamma mia," Chase muttered as they read a few excerpts together. "EL James should turn this into a book."

It confirmed that Wolf and Dany had been in a relationship, but nothing more. Odelia idly read through a few of the more recent exchanges while Chase dug through Wolf's closet, in search of something to tie the director to the murder.

Dany had been worried about Wolf's wife Emily, apparently, repeatedly asking Wolf how far along he was in his divorce procedure. Wolf kept assuring her he was going to file for divorce any day now, and she kept asking him to talk to his wife soon.

Finally, in the last message she'd sent him, she'd said, 'I don't know how much longer I'll be able to keep quiet. Each time I meet Emily I'm afraid I'm going to just blab it out!'

Odelia frowned. Wolf might have construed this as a threat. He might never have had any intention of divorcing his wife, who apparently was the source of his wealth and an important part of his business. So maybe he'd killed Dany before she could 'blab it out?'

Suddenly, she noticed Chase was wildly gesturing at her from the closet he was digging through. She hurried over, Wolf's phone still in her hand. When Chase stepped aside, she saw it: a yellow parka, tucked away in the far corner of his packed closet.

Chase gave her a meaningful look and took it out by the clothes hanger, careful not to touch the jacket itself. And the moment he did, she saw the tiny red dots that were spattered all across the front of the parka.

Blood.

Dany's blood.

☙

*D*ooley and I were walking back to the car when Harriet came walking up to us. Head hanging down, she didn't look like her usual feisty self.

"Hey, Max. Hey, Dooley,'" she said, and even sounded downcast.

"What's wrong?" I asked. "Where is Brutus?"

"Oh, around, I guess," she said, sounding as cheerful as a zombie who hasn't had their daily portion of brains.

Just then, there was a yelp followed by a scream, and then

we were running towards the source of the sound. I'd recognized the yelp as coming from Brutus, the scream as human in origin.

When we rounded the house, we discovered the scream had come from a small duck pond. What was it with duck ponds today? The pond itself was dwarfed by a rock wall that rose up like some jagged-edged monstrosity. The front was outfitted with climbing holds but the top hovered over that pond like a giant black beak.

When we arrived on the scene, a potbellied man was sitting on a bench, right beneath the promontory, looking dazed, with Brutus positioned squarely on his stomach.

"Brutus!" I cried. "What happened?"

"He-he saved me," said Brutus, staring at the man with some incredulity, as the man, equally flustered, was staring right back at him. "He just saved my life."

"Good thing you landed on my tummy, little buddy," said the man now. "Otherwise you'd have been nothing but a grease spot on this bench."

"See?" said Dooley. "My analogy was right on the money."

"Oh, shut up, Dooley," said Harriet. "Brutus?" she said croakily. "Are you all right?"

"I am now," he said. He looked shaken, not stirred, but otherwise in excellent fettle. The man, on the other hand, now pushed the black cat from his belly and rubbed it. He looked a little winded. Being hit by a falling Brutus would do that to a person, of course.

We all looked up, at the promontory thirty feet over our heads. It wouldn't have killed Brutus, and then again it might have.

"How the hell did you get up there?" I asked.

"I don't know. I was wandering, thinking, and suddenly... I was falling."

"The back of the wall must be a gentle slope down. Probably there's some kind of path leading from the top, so climbers can walk down once they've reached there," I said.

"This makes it the third time I almost died today," said Brutus with an uncharacteristic tremor in his voice. "Maybe I should just lock myself up in the house from now on, and stay put."

"Hey, that reminds me of those movies," said Dooley.

"What movies?" I said.

"Those *Final Destination* movies. A group of teenagers cheats death, and then death comes after them, killing them in increasingly freaky and horrible ways, one by one, until they're all dead, except for the token survivor, who gets it in the next movie."

"Dooley," I said, shaking my head. "Not now."

"But it's exactly the same thing!" He turned to Brutus. "Did you cheat death by any chance in the past couple of weeks?"

"I cheated death three times today," he said. He could have been white around the nostrils. It's hard to tell with a cat, what with all the fur.

"Mh," said Dooley, pensive. "In the movies death eventually gets them for sure. So maybe this is not your typical *Final Destination* case. Or maybe it is. In which case you'll die in a most excruciating but very cinematic and elaborate way in the next couple of hours."

"Oh, shut up, Dooley!" Harriet cried suddenly. "Why don't you just shut up for once!" And after this sudden outburst she ran off at a brisk pace, leaving us all a little puzzled.

"I guess she doesn't like movies," said Dooley.

Just then, all hell broke loose: the lights in the manor all lit up, and loud sirens of police cars on approach ripped through the nocturnal silence.

"Uh-oh," said Brutus. "I hope they're not here for me."

CHAPTER 26

*O*delia watched on as Wolf Langdon was led from the house and into a waiting squad car. He'd already professed his innocence several times, but it was hard to argue with the yellow parka covered in Dany's blood. When they'd finally woken him up and confronted him with the evidence, he'd been flabbergasted and had exclaimed, "That's not mine. That's not mine, I'm telling you! Someone put it there!" Even now, as he was being pushed into the car, he was screaming, "I'm being framed! You have to believe me! This is a setup!"

"Fat chance," said Chase. "Framed. Yeah, right." He bumped Odelia's fist. "Well done, babe. Your hunch paid off in spades." And then he walked off, to accompany Wolf to the station house for questioning.

Uncle Alec came waddling up to her. "I see my advice to stay out of this investigation was followed to the letter, huh?"

"I'm sorry, uncle. You know as well as I do it's hard to stay away from a case like this—especially when it involves someone I knew personally."

He nodded. "I guess I shouldn't have warned you off. I

124

should have known you'd ignore me. But what the hell were you and Chase doing in the man's bedroom?"

"Following a lead," she said. She explained about the message she'd seen on Wolf's phone, and how she'd decided to follow up on it.

"And a good thing you did." He scratched his scalp. "Now how am I going to explain your presence at the manor? You didn't happen to have a search warrant, did you?"

"Um…"

"Didn't think so," he muttered, then walked off after Chase, shaking his head and muttering something about meddling nieces under his breath.

Odelia just hoped the evidence wouldn't be thrown out of court because of this search warrant thingie.

At her feet, Max and Dooley had arrived, along with Brutus. Of Harriet no trace.

She squatted down and scratched her cats behind the ears. "You did well, guys. We caught the killer. This must be some kind of new record. Dany was killed this afternoon, and less than twelve hours later her killer is in police custody."

"I don't think he did it, though," said Max, surprising Odelia.

"What? What are you talking about?"

"Not what, who. We talked to Ringo."

"Who?"

"Ringo? Wolf's Chihuahua?"

"And a very nice doggie he is," Dooley added. "Just like you said."

"He told us Wolf was right by his side when Dany was killed."

"He witnessed the murder?"

"He did. He didn't see the killer's face, though."

"He did tell us to talk to Mr. Owl," said Dooley.

"Mr. Owl," she said dubiously.

"It's an owl that lives in the tree Dany was killed under," Max explained. "He must have seen the whole thing. We're hoping he'll give us a description of the killer."

"Can you take us to the park?" Dooley asked. "Owls are nocturnal creatures. Tomorrow he'll probably be asleep."

She threw up her hands. "I guess so." Sometimes she felt more like a taxi service for her cats than anything else. Then again, if Ringo was right, Wolf couldn't be the killer.

"But we found the yellow parka hanging in his closet. It still had Dany's blood all over it."

"The killer could have put it there," said Max.

"Or maybe Ringo is lying," she offered. "Have you considered that? He could be lying to protect Wolf." Max and Dooley surprised her by bursting out laughing. "What's so funny?"

"If you knew Ringo like we know him, you'd know he's incapable of lying."

"He's very naive," said Dooley. "Unlike us cats, dogs are very naive, trusting creatures."

Odelia turned to Brutus, who looked shell-shocked. "What's wrong with him?"

"Brutus had a near-death experience again," said Max. "The third in a row."

"I told him it's just like those *Final Destination* movies," said Dooley.

"Dooley," said Max warningly. "Not now."

"But it's true!"

"I fell to my death again," said Brutus, as if waking up from a stupor. "I was falling and falling and then I landed on something soft and squishy."

"A fat human," Dooley said.

"We don't call people fat, Dooley," said Odelia. "It's not a nice word."

"So what do we call them then?"

"Big-boned," said Odelia with a mischievous glance at Max.

Max frowned. "I'm big-boned. But would you call me fat?"

"You do tend to overindulge from time to time, Max," she said.

"Just like the guy who saved my life, and a good thing he does," said Brutus. He glanced around. "Um, where's Harriet?"

"I think she left," said Dooley.

"I saw her before she took off," said Max. "She said she was going for a walk. She needed to think and put some things into perspective."

"Perspective?" said Brutus. "Is that the word she used?"

Max nodded.

"Huh."

"Okay, you guys," said Odelia. "Let's go and see this Mr. Owl. It's late and I really need to catch some Z's."

CHAPTER 27

*O*delia parked her car near the entrance to the park, we all hopped out, and then were on our way to the notorious tree for our interview with an owl. I'd never talked to an owl before, and I was really looking forward to a tête-à-tête with one of these wise old birds.

There's just something about owls that tickles my imagination. They're fascinating creatures. Apart from that, they're also birds, of course, and for some reason cats are intrigued by birds as a rule. Not to eat them, mind you—though there are those amongst my species who will do anything to get their claws on a feathered friend—but to watch as they flit to and fro. In fact I can watch birds twitter and frolic in a tree for hours. I guess where humans love to people-watch, cats love to bird-watch. And we don't even need binoculars.

I'd told Odelia not to wait—that we'd find our own way home, and judging from the rattling sound her muffler made as she took off, she'd taken this advice to heart.

Parks, and perhaps other public places too, are quite different at night than during the day. Apart from the fact that lovers seem to flock to parks in the middle of the night —I'm referring to Hugh Grant and Julia Roberts in *Notting Hill*—there's a preternatural quiet that descends over a park once the sun decides to call it a night. A hush that lies over the area like a blanket. In jungles, nocturnal animals crawl out of their hiding places and create a symphony of sound. In parks? Nothing. Not even the hiss of a snake or the chirp of a cricket.

It's almost as if all of nature sleeps. Except cats, of course. We gather in the park for cat choir. And already, as we set paw for the tree where only hours before a young woman had met her tragic end, meows and screeches rent the air, and it was obvious that Shanille, cat choir's director, had gathered her troops and they were all giving of their best.

"Too bad we're missing cat choir because of this murder investigation," said Dooley, voicing my own thoughts exactly.

"That can't be a coincidence, can it?" said Brutus.

"What are you talking about, Brutus?" I asked.

"Perspective! She said she needed to get a little perspective. And all this time I've been telling her this whole thing is a matter of perspective. One big misunderstanding. Maybe she's finally starting to see things my way?"

"I wouldn't count on it," I said dryly. "Harriet sees things strictly her own way."

"But why would she use that particular word? Perspective?"

"Because that's what people do when they're faced with a personal crisis: they take a walk to get some perspective."

"Mh," said Brutus, not convinced.

It was obvious he'd started to hope against hope that Harriet would take him back. I could have told him this was a waste of time. Harriet was not one to be convinced by an argument. If Brutus wanted to win her back, he'd have to make a grand gesture. And since this was essentially the biggest crisis their relationship had faced since its inception, the grander the gesture the better. What gesture he should perform? I had no idea. I'm not an expert on feline love. And frankly I had other things on my mind. Like finding this owl.

We'd arrived at the old oak tree and stood gazing up at its majestic branches.

"Yoo-hoo," I hooted. "Mr. Owl? Could we please have a word? It's important."

No response. Not even a hoo-hoo-hoooooooo.

"I don't think he's home," said Dooley after we'd waited some more.

Cats have pretty sharp eyes, and I was inclined to agree with Dooley. I didn't detect any owl in this particular tree. It was, in other words, an owl-less tree.

"But where can he be? Ringo said he was sitting in this tree this afternoon—that this tree was his home."

"And how would Ringo know what tree Mr. Owl calls home?" Dooley argued. "Maybe he was just taking a little break from his usual tree and decided to try out this tree for size. And when this woman was murdered, he decided the tree was no good and he flew off again to sit in his own tree. Owls do fly, don't they?"

"They do," I said, still gazing up. I was getting a crick in the neck but I wasn't giving up. "Yoo-hoo," I tried again. "We're friends of Ringo. The Chihuahua who was here this afternoon? He says you saw the murder that took place under your tree. He also says you probably saw the killer's face. The thing is, we're not just your regular garden-variety cats. We're cat detectives. We detect. And right now we're detecting the murder of that poor young woman. So if you could help us out here, we'd be very much obliged."

"Oh, will you just shut up, already," suddenly an irritable voice sounded from up above. It wasn't the voice of God, at least I didn't think so. So it was probably Mr. Owl.

"Mr. Owl," I said, much relieved. "Is that you up there?"

"Please stop calling me Mr. Owl. I'm a lady not a gentleman. And if you dare call me Mrs. Owl I'm going to swoop down and bite you."

"So what do we call you?"

"Rita," she said after a moment's hesitation.

"Great!" I said. "So, how about it, Rita? Can you help us out here?"

"I don't know," she said. "You're cats."

No argument there. We were cats. "That's right."

"So this is probably just a trick to get me to come out of this tree. And then you'll pounce on me and eat me. So no can do, cat. Please go away, and don't come back."

"We would never pounce on you and eat you," said Dooley. "Isn't that right, Max?"

"Of course not. We're not those kind of cats."

"What are you talking about? You're cats. Cats eat birds. I'm a bird. This is not rocket science. So take a hike, will you? You ain't sweet-talking me out of this tree."

"Like I said, we're not like that," I said. "We, um—"

"We're vegetarians," said Dooley.

Both Brutus and I stared at Dooley, who smiled winningly.

"Vegetarians. Really," said Rita. She obviously wasn't buying it.

"Yeah, that's right," I said, deciding to go with the flow. "Meat is murder, right?"

"So what do you eat?" she challenged.

"Um…" I cast about for a good alternative to meat. "Brown rice?"

"Yummy," said Dooley, while Brutus winced.

"What else?" asked Rita. "What's your favorite food?"

"Um... lentils?" I offered, though I could already feel my stomach churning.

"I like tofu," said Dooley. "I can eat tofu for breakfast, lunch and dinner."

"And what do *you* like, black cat?" asked Rita, still not convinced.

"I like, um, broccoli," said Brutus, then gulped. "And quinoa."

Silence reigned for a few moments while Rita considered this. There was a soft rustle, and she flew into view, taking perch on a lower branch. She was a big bird. Big and fluffy. She looked pretty yummy to me. I'd sworn to Odelia I'd never eat birds, though, and I intended to keep my promise. Brutus, though, who'd never made such a promise, stared at Rita, and already I could hear his stomach growl and see his eyes glaze over. We were all hungry, not having eaten in hours, and a juicy bird like Rita would have hit the spot just fine.

Instead, I said, "So. Can you tell us what happened here this afternoon?"

"Not much to tell," said Rita. "A man stabbed a woman and left her to die. Happens all the time." She shook her head. "Humans. They're probably the most murderous species ever to roam this earth. Though Tyrannosaurus Rexes were no picnic either."

I decided to ignore the philosophical musings and get right down to brass tacks. "Did you get a good look at the killer's face?"

"Sure. He had a human face. That's because he was a human," she said, very logically, I thought.

"So, what did he look like?"

We all waited with bated breath for her response. This was the moment of the big reveal. The moment we'd all been waiting for. The moment we were going to learn the identity of the killer.

"How should I know?" said Rita. "Humans all look the same to me."

Ugh. So she was one of those owls, huh?

"Yeah, they do look alike, but there are differences," I pointed out. "Some humans have big noses, others have small noses. Some have freckles, some don't. Some have blond hair, others have brown hair, some even have blue hair..."

She frowned, or at least I thought she did. Like with cats and fur, it's tough to read between the feathers. "Well, he had a regular nose, I guess. Nothing to write home about. Regular face, regular build, regular mouth, regular arms, regular—"

"What color was his hair?"

"He wore one of those caps, with the bill covering the upper portion of his face."

"Did he have a beard, mustache..."

"No beard, no mustache."

"Color of his eyes?"

"Sunglasses," she said with a shrug.

Dang it. "So what can you tell us about him? Any distinguishing features?"

She thought hard, then spread her wings. "I don't know, all right? What is this? A third-degree? Why is this so important, anyway? Plenty of humans get killed all the time."

"It's important because Dany Cooper was a friend of our human."

"Yeah, you may think humans all enjoy killing each other but that's simply not true," said Dooley. "Our human is a very nice human and she would never kill anyone. She just wouldn't. In fact she dedicates her life to finding those nasty humans who do kill others."

"It's also against the law," said Brutus. "The human law, that is."

"Well…" The owl hesitated. "He did have one distinguishing feature that I thought was a little weird."

"What was it?" I asked, suddenly excited again.

"He had an owl-shaped mole on the back of his hand, which I personally found insulting."

"An owl-shaped mole?"

"Yup. On his right hand—the hand he stabbed the woman with. Very inappropriate. I mean, I admit to enjoying a nice, juicy mouse from time to time, but I'd never kill a fellow owl. That's just so… human."

"You're right," I said. "Only humans kill other humans."

"That's not entirely true, though," said Dooley, surprising us. "There are plenty of species that kill their own. In fact the most murderous mammal species are meerkats. Meerkats kill twenty percent of their own kind."

"Interesting," I said, wondering why, oh why I had ever extolled the virtues of the Discovery Channel. He wasn't finished, though. Like a real professor, he just droned on.

"It is true, however, that most mammal murders involve infanticide—the killing of babies. In meerkat society it's the dominant female who routinely murders the pups of the subordinate females in their own group. Humans are part of a small group of mammals—among them lions, wolves and spotted hyenas—that routinely murder the adults of their own species. And of course humans are very creative to find ways to kill each other. Lions or wolves or spotted hyenas will never use poison or guns or knives or whatever to kill other lions or wolves or spotted hyenas."

"That's fine, Dooley," I muttered.

"You're very smart, for a cat," said Rita appreciatively.

"One of Gran's soaps is on hiatus so I've been watching the Discovery Channel."

"I can tell," I said.

At any rate, we'd gotten what we'd come here to find.

Now all we needed to do was find out if Wolf Langdon had a mole on his hand in the shape of an owl. If he had, Ringo had been lying to us when he said Wolf was standing right next to him when Dany was killed.

We thanked Rita profusely and I like to think that we left her with the impression that not all cats are vicious bird-eaters.

"I only wish more cats were like you!" she said. "Vegetarians, I mean."

We took our leave, and as we walked away, Brutus said, "I hate broccoli. And quinoa."

"And I hate lentils," I said.

"I actually like tofu," said Dooley. "I think I could get used to it."

"It's all matter of perspective," I said with a grin.

Brutus didn't even crack a smile.

Probably too soon.

CHAPTER 28

*A*s she was driving home, Odelia got a message from her uncle.

'If you're going to inject yourself into this investigation, you might as well drop down to the station to watch the interview.'

She smiled, performed a quick U-turn and headed down to the station. She didn't particularly enjoy police interviews, but she did want to see what Wolf had to say for himself. Even though her cats were pretty convinced the director had nothing to do with Dany's murder, the presence of that yellow parka in his closet proved otherwise. As Chase had said, it was an open-and-shut case. One of those cases where the killer is so cocky he trips up even before the person he murdered has arrived at the morgue.

She parked in front of the station house and quickly hurried inside, not even bothering to lock up her car. The pickup was so old and decrepit no one in their right mind would steal it.

She arrived at the interview room at the back of the

station, and when she entered found her uncle already standing at the two-way mirror.

He looked up when she entered. "I thought you'd want to see this."

"Thanks, uncle," she said, and gave his shoulder a squeeze.

"I know it's hopeless to try and keep you from putting your sleuth cap on, but you can't blame me for trying," he said in response. "Especially considering how much the victim resembled you."

"Well, you were wrong about me being the killer's target."

"It would appear so," he said cautiously.

She thought about Brutus almost being run over, but decided not to mention the fact. That was probably a coincidence. There was, after all, probably more than one person dressed in a yellow parka driving around Hampton Cove.

In the interview room, Chase and Wolf sat, the director uncharacteristically ill at ease. His hair was a mess, and so was his beard, and he was still dressed in his silk pajamas.

"I didn't do it, detective!" he exclaimed. "You have to believe me! I liked that girl. She had a gift. Why would I kill a promising young talent like that!"

"I'll tell you exactly why," said Chase, who was his usual unruffled self. He was never better than when interviewing suspects and making them sweat. "You were having an affair with Dany Cooper, and when she pressured you into getting a divorce from your wife, you knew it was time to get rid of her."

"That's... crazy," blustered Don. "Who told you that?"

"You told me yourself." Chase placed Wolf's own phone on the table and tapped it. "I've made a printout of your WhatsApp chats. Pretty hot stuff, Mr. Langdon."

Wolf's face turned white as a sheet. "I thought WhatsApp messages were automatically deleted?"

"That's Snapchat. You should probably read up on your social media. Now do you still deny having an affair with Miss Cooper?"

He hung his head. "No, I don't," he said, now with a voice as if from the tomb. "We were having an affair. It's true." He looked up. "But I didn't kill her."

Chase took a stack of papers he'd brought into the interview room and began reading. "Wolfy, baby. Have you talked to your wife yet? Inquiring minds want to know. Smiley smiley smiley. When is the divorce planned? Heart heart heart. I think I can hear the wedding bells already. Kiss kiss kiss. Can't wait to say I do, sweet boo. Cupid Cupid Cupid."

"All right, all right, all right," said Wolf. "Yes. I promised her I'd divorce Emily."

"But you were never going to do that. Because your wife was your partner in Langdon Productions, and without her and her family's money, you were sunk."

"Who told you all this?" Then he shook his head. "Never mind. You're right. I couldn't get a divorce. Not unless my next couple of projects all proved sure-fire hits. Emily had already told me she was sick and tired of throwing good money after bad. Called the production company a black hole. So it was do or die, and the Bard in the Park thing in the Hamptons was going to give me a lot of publicity and hopefully push my next Broadway show, which I'm hoping will put us in the black. And I promised Dany the main part." He spread his arms. "So you see? I would never kill her. She was going to be my star."

"So why didn't you give her the starring role in Bard in the Park?"

"Like I said, I'm only doing these Bard in the Park shows for the visibility and the buzz. There's no money in it. Plus, I didn't want to show off Dany and risk her being wooed away by the competition when they saw how good she was. And she was awesome."

Odelia frowned. So what did that make her? Less than awesome, apparently.

"You're not making your case here, Wolf. You just admitted you couldn't afford to get divorced. And that Dany was pressuring you. So why don't you simply admit you killed her?"

"But I didn't! I loved that kid. She was great fun to be around. And I'm the one who discovered her. This was just like that movie..." He snapped his fingers. "*A Star Is Born!*"

"In *A Star Is Born* the male commits suicide when the female's success eclipses his own," said Chase dryly.

"What I mean to say is, I discovered her. I was going to turn her into a star, and—"

"And then you were going to ride on the coattails of her success."

"Exactly!" said Wolf without a trace of irony. "She was my ticket to the big time. If she became a star, I didn't need Emily or her damn money. I could buy her out. Be my own man!" He tapped the table frantically. "So why would I kill Dany, huh? It makes no sense!"

Odelia turned to her uncle. "Max and Dooley talked to Wolf's Chihuahua."

Uncle Alec grinned. "Now there's something you don't hear every day."

She ignored him. "The dog—who is called Ringo, by the way—said Wolf would never kill Dany. They had a good thing going, but also, Wolf was with Ringo when Dany was killed. He saw the killer, Alec. He saw the killer and it wasn't Wolf Langdon."

Uncle Alec fingered one of his chins. "Are you sure about this?"

"Yes. Ringo also said he didn't get a good look at the killer's face, but an owl did."

Alec's grin widened. "An owl."

"An owl, yes. Sitting in a tree..." Hearing herself, she had to smile, too. It sounded pretty ridiculous. "Anyway, Max and Dooley are talking to this owl as we speak, so..."

Uncle Alec nodded. "You think we may have arrested the wrong guy."

"Could be. Unless the dog is lying, but in my experience dogs rarely lie."

That grin was back.

"Yes, I know how this sounds," she said. "But you know me, uncle. I've solved cases you thought were unsolvable before."

"I know you have. And I'll be happy to hear what this... owl has to say. In the meantime Wolf Langdon is still my best suspect, and I'm keeping him right here."

"The yellow parka."

"The yellow parka—and his motive. Greed is always a great motive for murder, and he had a whopper of a motive, no matter what he's saying about this *A Storm Is Born* stuff."

She didn't bother to correct him. "Someone could have planted that parka."

"Someone could have, but in *my* experience that is rarely the case."

"So what about the Chihuahua and the owl?"

He held up his hand. "I know your Dr. Dolittle qualities have been useful on more than one occasion, honey, but the statement of a dog and an owl is not something that will stand up in court, I'm afraid. A solid motive and physical evidence, on the other hand..."

"I understand," she said.

"Besides. Just like humans sometimes make lousy witnesses, so can dogs. Or owls."

She glanced back at Wolf, who was still trying to convince Chase of his innocence.

Looked like her career as an actress was finished before it even started.

CHAPTER 29

*T*he next day, Tex was on his way to work when suddenly a flowerpot crashed down onto the pavement right in front of him. One fraction of a second later, and he'd have gotten it straight on the noggin. It was a heavy flowerpot, as flowerpots go, and would have crushed his skull and sent him to an early grave if the thing had hit its intended target.

Intended target?

Even while his heart was still beating a snare drum inside his chest, Tex wondered why the thought had occurred to him that this was no random flowerpot incident but a concerted effort to make him dead. In other words, an attempt on his life.

He glanced down at the flowerpot, which now rested beyond repair at his feet, sand and a wilted undefinable plant spilling out beyond the shards. Then he looked up to determine the source of the phenomenon. A windowsill on the third floor of an adjacent building was the likely resting place of the pot before it had decided to take the sudden leap into the unknown. And just as he looked, he thought he saw that very same window that was framed by that very same ledge, gently being closed by an unseen hand.

His face took on a more determined expression. "Hey!" he shouted, balling his fist at the now-closed window. "I saw you! Don't think for a minute I didn't see you! What's the big idea, chucking flowerpots at innocent passersby?"

And in a sudden wave of indignation, he turned to the house whose window had been used for this dastardly murder attempt, and rattled its handle. Locked, of course. But no worries. The culprit who'd done this dastardly deed no doubt was still inside.

"Let's see you get away with this," Tex muttered, as he took out his phone. He called up his brother-in-law's number and hit Connect. The moment Alec picked up, he bellowed, "Alec! Someone just tried to kill me! That's right. And I've got the killer locked up in the house! He's not getting away. You better do what it is you do—arrest him! Arrest him, man!"

Five minutes later, three police vehicles descended on the scene, sirens wailing, and six police officers exited and one ruddy-looking police chief. Alec was panting. An attack on his brother-in-law in his own town was not something that happened every day, nor was it something he was willing to overlook.

"Where is he?" he said between two gulping breaths as he came hurrying up. He dragged up his pants, which, in spite of his sturdy belt, always seemed to be sagging, and glanced up at the house Tex was pointing a rigid finger at.

"He's still inside. I'm sure of it. I've been here all this time and he hasn't come out."

"What did he do? Take a shot at you?"

"Worse! He dropped a flowerpot on my head!"

Alec blinked. "A flowerpot?"

"A flowerpot!"

And to prove he wasn't making this up, he pointed at the evidence.

Alec stared at the remnants of the flowerpot which now lay in ruins.

"So who was he?"

"Mh?"

"The guy who threw the pot at you?"

"I have no idea. He's locked himself inside and he won't come out. And don't think I haven't tried. I must have rung the bell a million times. I even pounded the door."

Alec gestured to his troops. "Break down this door. And use extreme caution. There's a killer inside."

His officers wasted no time and had the door down within seconds, using a nifty device that looked like something the Assyrians would have used to attack an enemy city. It was called a battering ram, Alec said, which seemed appropriate. Tex wasn't interested in the nomenclature or the technical details of the operation, though. All he wanted was to see justice done and this killer taken into custody so he could never flowerpotbomb anyone ever again.

Five minutes later, the police officers came walking out of the building. One after the other, they shook their heads.

"No one?" asked Tex, incredulous.

"Not a single person inside," said the last officer to exit the house. "And we searched the place top to bottom. There was a window open on the second floor, though, so the culprit may have escaped through there. It's only a six foot drop onto the roof of a shack of some kind, and we found several footprints right next to it."

"Make sure you photograph those prints," Alec ordered.

"Yes, sir," said the cop, and returned into the house to carry out the boss's orders.

Alec scratched his head. "One question, Tex."

"Shoot."

"Are you sure you saw someone chuck this pot at you?"

"Of course I'm sure! I saw the window close myself."

"So can you describe this flowerpot chucker to me?"

"Eh?"

"What did he look like?" He'd taken out his little note-book and was hovering pencil over paper, ready to take down Tex's detailed description.

"Well, I didn't see his face, of course. By the time I looked up, he was gone."

Alec frowned. "You didn't see his face."

"Of course not. I was too busy reeling from the shock. Have you ever had a flowerpot aimed at your head? No? Then you have no idea how terrible it feels. Your heart races, you see your whole life flash by in an instant, your blood pressure spikes…" Speaking of blood pressure, he now pressed his index finger against his jugular and checked his watch.

Alec used his pencil to scratch his scalp. "So how do know it was a he?"

"Eh?" Blood pressure seemed normal. Under the circum-stances, of course.

"How do you know—"

"I heard you the first time. Well, why wouldn't it be a he? I can't imagine a woman throwing a flowerpot at an innocent passerby. Men are more prone to violence. Everybody knows that. And don't you remember how Brutus almost got run over by that man in the yellow parka yesterday? Obviously someone is targeting this family, Alec, and obviously this person is a man. The same man who killed that poor girl that looked so much like Odelia."

"I don't—"

Tex did a double take. "Do you think he may have made a mistake? That he wanted to kill Odelia but he killed this Dany Cooper girl instead?"

145

"I don't think—"

He tapped Alec's chest sharply. "That means Odelia might still be in danger, Alec! You must send a unit round to her house at once. On the double!"

"I don't think there's any chance of that, Tex."

"And why is that?"

"Because we caught Dany Cooper's killer last night. He's in custody and he won't kill again."

This had Tex stumped for a moment. He was, after all, a doctor, not a cop, and these glimpses into the inner workings of a police department sometimes confused him. Then something occurred to him. He tapped Alec's chest again, making the other man wince. "Have you considered that you may have arrested the wrong man?"

"The wrong man?"

"Of course! If the killer is in custody, how do you explain him chucking flowerpots at me?!"

CHAPTER 30

*G*ran was on her way to work when she noticed that her son-in-law and a whole bunch of cops stood gabbing away across the street. She liked to leave a few minutes after Tex, because she didn't want him to think of her as a mere employee doing his bidding. She might have accepted to work at his doctor's office as a favor to Tex, but that didn't mean she was his underling. She was her own person and not a flunky to be ordered around by Tex.

It had always been Vesta's opinion that a son-in-law should be kept on a short leash, and a very short one at that. So when she saw Tex having a nice chat with Alec while they should be working, she didn't even bother to join them. If Tex wanted to spend his time chatting instead of putting in the hours he owed his patients, that was his business. She would make sure she showed up first, and tell the patients the doctor had been delayed.

Or she could put in a quick stop at the deli and pick up some of that strawberry cream chocolate she liked so much. Or maybe she'd get the caramel cream one. And as she pondered this all-important decision, she suddenly stepped on a roller skate, which, true to form, slipped from under her and she fell, hard, on the pavement. And just as she did, she caught a glimpse of something yellow streak past in the front yard of the adjacent house.

Immediately, she started screaming bloody murder. Moments later, Tex, Alec and the entirety of the Hampton Cove Police Department came hopping to.

"Ma!" Alec cried, taking her left arm. "Are you all right?"

"What happened?" asked Tex, grabbing her right arm. Together, they hoisted her up.

"Someone put that skate there on purpose!" she exclaimed, pointing at the offending skate.

"Are you sure?" asked Alec.

"Of course I'm sure. What kind of question is that! I saw him! He was dressed in yellow and he ran that way." When no one moved, she yelled, "Don't just stand there! Go after him!"

And after him they went, all cops except for Alec and Tex, who wasn't a cop but a doctor, and was now examining her for possible fractures.

She yanked her arm from his grasp. "Oh, I'm all right. It takes more than a nasty killer to get the better of me."

"So you saw him too, huh?" said Tex, who looked shaken.

It was too much to say that her son-in-law's sudden concern touched Gran's heart, such as it was, but it did give her a twinge of satisfaction. She'd obviously trained Tex well, for him to suddenly display these signs of affection towards his sweet old mother-in-law.

"Yeah, I saw him. Dressed in yellow. A real fiend, to leave a skate like that. He must have known I'd trip over it and hoped I'd break my neck, being the old lady that I am. Old ladies easily break their necks, you see, on account of the fact that their bones are brittle and stuff. Not my bones, though. He hadn't counted on that, the piece of skunk that he is."

Alec was studying the skate. "Are you sure it wasn't just kids that left this thing?"

"Of course I'm sure! Odelia told me about the killer dressed in yellow who killed her lookalike. Then Tex saves poor Brutus from the same killer. And now the killer tried to kill me! It's an outrage he's still running around free! What the heck do I pay taxes for?"

"You don't pay taxes, Ma," said Alec, the wise-ass. "You're retired."

"I'm a working woman. Of course I pay taxes!"

"You're a volunteer. I don't pay you," said Tex.

"What?! I work for free?! That's an outrage! I'm going to the union, you cheapskate!"

"I pay you a little something under the table." He made a weird move with his hand, as if scooping up a pancake. "Get it? Under the table? Besides, I give you room and board."

"I get that you're exploiting a poor old lady, you robber baron. Wait till the union is through with you. You'll be happy if they leave you so much as a cardboard box to sleep in."

"Tex thinks he was attacked, too," said Alec, returning to the point.

"I don't *think* I was attacked. I *was* attacked. By the same killer who attacked Vesta."

"See?" said Gran. "Even Tex was attacked, and he's probably Odelia's least favorite family member."

Tex stared at her. "Come again?"

"Isn't it obvious? This killer is targeting the people Odelia cares about the most. He attacked the girl, the actress, to make sure he got Odelia's attention, then he attacked Brutus —probably because Max wasn't available—and now he attacked me, the favorite. Next he'll attack Marge, and he was going to keep you for last, Tex. My best guess is that he probably saw you passing by and figured why the hell not strike while the flowerpot is hot?"

Alec and Tex exchanged a glance. "Marge!" they both exclaimed simultaneously.

Alec searched around for his officers and cursed under his breath. They were all gone, of course, having followed his orders to track down Vesta's roller skate killer.

"You should really discipline your people, Alec," said Gran. "You can't just let them wander off like that when you need them the most."

But Alec was already running away, along with Tex, in the direction of the library, Marge's place of employment.

"Nice," Gran grumbled. "Talk about victim assistance. Leaving a poor old lady to deal with the trauma of her near-death experience all by herself." But then the significance of her own words came home to her, and she muttered, "Marge. Oh, dammit." And as fast as her sticks for legs could carry her, she was off in the direction of the library, too.

CHAPTER 31

*M*arge was stocking Danielle Steel books, enjoying these rare moments of quiet before the library opened. She loved her job, and had been a big library fan even as a child, finding herself here almost daily. Her folks used to drop her and Alec off at the library when they went into town to shop, and little Marge found plenty of books to keep her busy until their return. Alec had a tougher time finding something to occupy his time. He'd never been a big reader, and even now preferred watching ESPN to picking up something to read.

To work in the place that had offered Marge so many fun memories was a dream come true. And even though the library was small—basically a one-woman operation—she didn't mind. She had plenty of opportunities to socialize as she knew pretty much every single person who came into the library. As a long-time resident of Hampton Cove she knew everyone in town, and never stinted for conversation with her steady set of regulars.

The first people through the door every morning were what she called her old-timers, who were already waiting before she opened the doors, and who headed straight for the reading room, where all the important national and local newspapers and magazines were stocked. The second most favorite station was the bank of internet computers, where those who didn't have internet at home came to check their email or surf the web.

Marge had taken a crash course in computers and the Internet just to handle all the requests from people not habituated to working with these machines. She sometimes joked she was part IT person, part psychologist, and part literary critic, as people relied on her to advise them on what to take home as reading material.

And since she knew her customers, she unfailingly picked the right book for them.

She checked her watch. Ten to nine. Time to open her up.

She liked to open early, and didn't mind if she closed late. It wasn't as if she was running an army barracks. This was Hampton Cove, and she ran a pretty relaxed ship.

Speaking of ships, she decided to quickly check the pirate ship that was the hallmark of the kids' section. The boat, which was a reading space made up to look like an actual pirate ship, was very popular with the younger readers. Marge had placed cushions on the seats, and there were plenty of nooks and crannies where kids could curl up with a book, just the way she herself had done when she was their age.

And she was just fluffing up one of the pillows when suddenly there was a creaking sound just over her head. When she looked up, she detected movement where no movement should have been. She jumped clear of the ship just in time before she was crushed by whatever had come loose. And as she lay there, a little dazed, she saw that it was the ship's mast, which had come crashing down. If she hadn't had the reflexes to jump when she had, she would have been seriously injured or worse. That mast was pretty heavy.

From inside the library, there was a loud commotion. She pushed herself to her feet and staggered to the main part of the library. When she saw that her brother Alec was pounding on the door, along with Tex, her husband, fear suddenly gripped her heart. She hurried over, her cheeks flushed, and turned the key in the lock as fast as she could. She yanked open the door and cried, "Odelia! Did something happen to Odelia?!"

"Odelia is fine," said Alec, instantly understanding her fear. He put his hand on her arm. "How about you? Are you all right?"

"Well, something did just almost fall on top of me, but apart from that I'm fine. Why? What's going on?"

Tex fixed her with an intent look. "Did you see a man with a yellow parka?"

She shook her head. "No. It's just me in here. Why? Did something happen?" She remembered the man with the yellow parka being mentioned in that horrible murder of that girl Odelia worked with, as well as in connection to the man who almost ran over Brutus.

Just then, Vesta came running up, panting like a horse after the Preakness Stakes.

"Marge! Thank God! It's the man in the yellow parka! He's coming for us! He tried to kill me!"

"And me," said Tex.

"You said something fell on top of you," said Alec, looking grim. "Can you show me?"

She led them to the back, and when Mom and Tex saw the wreckage, they both gasped. Alec's frown deepened, as he crouched down with some effort to study the wreckage. Finally he looked up. "I'm not an expert but it looks like this has been tampered with."

"What do you mean?" asked Marge, horrified.

He pointed to the mast. "This has been sawn clear through."

"Oh, my God," said Marge. "The children. Someone could have gotten killed!"

"You almost got killed," said Tex, and drew her in for a bracing hug.

"We're under attack," said Gran seriously. "We have to warn Odelia. She needs police protection." She looked at Alec. "We all do."

CHAPTER 32

*O*delia had gotten up late. By the time she opened her eyes, Chase had already left for work. She groaned. She must have forgotten to set her alarm last night. Then again, it had been pretty late, so the extra sleep had been welcome.

At her feet, her cats were dozing, or at least Max and Dooley were. Of Brutus, there was no trace, and neither of Harriet.

She stretched and yawned. Time to get up and start a new day.

She smiled to herself as she recalled her dream. Chase had finally taken her out on a date. It was a running joke between them that every time they arranged to go out for dinner and a movie, something happened to make sure they didn't get to the end of their date.

That was the problem when a cop and a reporter dated: some crisis always cropped up.

She didn't mind. At least in her dream they'd gone to see the movie and had actually managed to watch it until the end. It was a Nancy Meyers movie, not exactly the kind of movie Chase would like, which also showed her it had been a dream, and not a memory.

Then another memory stirred: Max telling her about their meeting with the owl, and the owl telling them about the killer's birthmark. But since she vividly remembered Wolf Langdon having a birthmark on his right hand, that had sealed the deal for her.

Ringo had been mistaken: his master hadn't been right next to him. His master had been murdering Dany Cooper, and either Ringo hadn't recognized Wolf from behind, or he'd purposely lied to protect him.

Which wasn't a big surprise. Pets would often do whatever they could to protect their humans. She knew Max would do anything for her, and so would Dooley.

So the case was closed, and all that remained was to write a front-page article detailing the nocturnal bust, and interview the people involved. She hoped her uncle would help her get access to Wolf so she could interview him in prison. Maybe to her he'd finally admit what he'd done, and they could put this whole terrible episode behind them.

Max opened his eyes and yawned, which triggered another bout of yawns from her and Dooley, who'd also woken up.

"Where is Chase?" asked Max.

She smiled. It was adorable how quickly her cats had warmed to her boyfriend.

"Gone to work. Where are Brutus and Harriet?"

"No idea. Brutus was with us when we came home last night, but of Harriet no trace."

"She said she needed to get some perspective," said Dooley. "I don't know what perspective is, but it sure seems to take her a long time to find it."

"Perspective is a state of mind," Odelia explained,

throwing off the covers and slipping her feet into her Hello Kitty slippers.

"A state of mind?"

"Harriet probably meant she wants to sort out some stuff in her life." Perhaps the Brutus thing, Odelia thought. She hoped they would be able to settle in a new amicable relationship. Otherwise it would be very unpleasant for the others if two cats kept on fighting and bickering. If worse came to worst, she'd have to have a talk with Harriet and Brutus herself. Clear the air. Play cat therapist.

She walked over to the window and yanked the curtains wide to let the sun stream in. From her window she had a great view of the backyards of all the neighboring houses. Nearby was a middle school, and she could hear the kids playing the moment she cracked open the window. A church spire gleamed in the distance, and she took a deep breath. A new day, and a fresh beginning. And she was just running a few scenarios through her mind on how to arrange her day, when suddenly her phone started buzzing, and buzzing, and buzzing some more. She frowned as she picked it up. Messages from her uncle, her mother, her dad, and her grandmother rolled across the screen, one after the other.

'Where are you?'

'Are you all right?'

'Answer me!'

What was going on?

She picked up the phone and called up her mom's number and was just about to hit Connect when she slipped over the bedside rug and went down hard, hitting her head against the bed as she did. The last thing she remembered was Max, yelling, "Odeliaiaaaah!"

And then the world went dark.

*I*t was by far the scariest thing I'd ever encountered. One minute I was chatting happily with my human, the next she went down and was gone. The phone slipped from her hand, bounced three times on the hardwood floor, and then kept sliding across the floor, buzzing all the while with incoming messages.

Both Dooley and I gathered around Odelia, and I watched in horror as a trickle of blood seeped from her temple.

"Is she dead?" asked Dooley in a choked voice.

"I don't know! What do we do?"

"We have to wake her up," said Dooley. "Make sure she stays awake. If she closes her eyes, she's a goner."

"Her eyes are closed already!" Nevertheless, I pawed her face. "Odelia, wake up," I said urgently. "Odelia! Can you hear me?!"

Oh, this was bad. This was very, very bad.

I lifted an eyelid, but all I found was a deadish-looking eye staring back at me.

"I think she's dead," I said, and stifled a panicky sob.

"We have to do what humans do," said Dooley. "Call 911."

"And how do you suppose we do that?!"

We both stared at Odelia's phone, which was still buzzing away.

'How hard can it be?" said Dooley. "It's a touchscreen. So let's touch it."

We moved over to the phone and stared at the thing. Then I gathered my courage and flicked it to life. Messages flashed across the screen. I ignored them. Instead, I called up the phone app, then tapped 911 and hit the Connect button.

"Now what?" I asked.

"Now you tell them Odelia may be dead or dying and to get here immediately!"

A woman's voice intoned, "Nine one one, what's your emergency?"

I yelled, in case she couldn't hear me, "You have to come quick. Odelia has bumped her head and she's not responding! There's also blood!"

"Sir or ma'am, I can't hear a thing on account of the fact that your cat is meowing. Please remove your animal and tell me what your emergency is."

"It's Odelia!" I tried again. "Send an ambulance! Quick!"

"I have to advise you once again to remove your cat. I can't hear a thing with all the meowing."

"Help!" Dooley cried. "Help!"

"I can't believe this," the woman said, sounding annoyed, and just hung up!

"I don't think she understood us," said Dooley.

"I think you're right," I said.

There was only one thing we could do, and that was to get help.

So we both ran from the room and down the stairs, then out through the cat flap and into the backyard. First destination: Marge. She wasn't home, of course, having gone to the library. So we ran out into the street, on our way to the library. Marge would understand. She would call 911 and tell that silly woman that there was an emergency.

We hadn't even run a hundred yards when a strange sight greeted our eyes: Uncle Alec, Tex, Marge and Gran all came huffing and puffing around the corner, as if they'd just run a marathon. When they saw us, they all started talking at the same time, and so did Dooley and I.

Finally, I managed to shout, "It's Odelia! She took a nasty fall and she looks dead!"

That urged them into action, and soon they were galloping towards the house.

"It's the man in the yellow parka," Gran huffed as she passed us. "He's done it again!"

I hadn't seen any man in a yellow parka. Just Odelia slipping on the rug. But Gran seemed sure of herself, and there was no time to argue, so I kept my mouth shut.

At the house, they all stomped up the stairs, and so did we.

Tex sank down on his knees next to his daughter, pressed his fingers into her neck and quickly said, his voice quaking with emotion, "She's alive. She's alive!"

They all laughed with relief, and so did Dooley and I. Funny how your life can change in the blink of an eye, and how a few words can bring you from the depths of despair back to the surface.

"She just had a nasty bump," Tex said, examining her further. "We need to get her to a hospital, though, just in case. She might have a concussion."

Soon the humans in the room took control of the situation, an ambulance was called in, and moments later a car screeched to a stop in front of the house, and another heavy body came stomping up the stairs. It was Chase. The moment he saw an inert and pale Odelia, he bellowed, "Odelia, no!"

"She's fine," said Tex, putting a hand on the cop's arm. "She slipped and fell but she'll be fine. I'll stake my reputation on it."

Chase sank down on the floor next to Odelia and took her hand. He now looked as pale as she did, and I wondered why that was. Low blood pressure, maybe. Or blood sugar? Someone should probably have offered him candy. He looked like he was about to faint.

The sound of an ambulance reached my finely tuned ears, and moments later the humans picked up the sound, too, for they all looked very much relieved.

Then Gran turned to me and Dooley. "There's one thing I need to know from you guys," she said sternly. "And don't you dare lie to me."

I saw how Chase was watching on, a puzzled look on his face.

"Was the man in yellow involved in this 'accident?'" She used her fingers to make air quotes.

"There was no man in yellow," I said.

"There was a yellow carpet, though," said Dooley. "It made Odelia slip and fall."

Gran narrowed her eyes at us. "You're sure about that?"

We both nodded.

"Huh," she said, as if she hadn't expected that. "How weird is that?"

Chase shook his head. Luckily Gran has a reputation for being slightly unhinged, so he probably didn't think much of her talking to us. Besides, he had other things to deal with, now that the paramedics came galloping up the stairs, a stretcher dangling between them. They quickly scooped Odelia up, then carried her down the stairs, with some grunts and groans. And as we watched on, she was loaded into the waiting ambulance, Marge and Tex joining them while Chase jumped into his pickup and took off after the ambulance.

"What a morning," said Alec once they were gone. "What. A. Morning."

"You can say that again," I said, even though Alec couldn't understand.

CHAPTER 33

*B*rutus had heard the commotion, but he'd opted not to get involved. He had enough problems of his own to contend with to get mixed up in the ongoing human drama that seemed to be an important part of life at the Pooles. He was sitting in one of his favorite spots in the world: the rosebushes at the back of Odelia's backyard. It was here that he and Harriet had always used to sit. Here that they'd spent some of the best moments in their love affair, and it was here that Brutus decided to come to cherish those sweet memories.

Also, he'd had three brushes with death already, and wasn't looking for a fourth.

So no more ponds for him, or high places where all he could do was stumble off and hope there was someone to break his fall. This time he was going to stay in his beloved rosebushes and dream of his beloved Harriet.

And as he dreamed, he thought he could almost hear her voice. He'd closed his eyes and imagined things could go back to the way they were before the incident. And as he thought about Darlene, he suddenly had a sinking feeling.

And then he realized that he was actually sinking. For real.

He opened his eyes and realized the ground was swallowing him up!

He was sinking faster and faster. Nearby, he thought he could hear Harriet shouting, "Brutus!" But that was just his imagination, of course. Why would Harriet be shouting his name like that? Not in anger, as she had for the past two days, but in anguish, almost as if she were watching him sinking deeper and deeper.

And even as the ground kept swallowing him up, he thought that this was probably the way it had to be. Life seemed adamant on casting him into these dangerous situations, so maybe this was the punishment he deserved.

"Brutus!" Harriet shouted.

This time it sounded even closer.

"Hold on! I'm going to try something!"

"Harriet? Is that you?"

But it couldn't be. She wasn't talking to him.

"Don't give up, Brutus!"

"Is that really you?"

The muddy muck he was sinking into was up to his chest now, and he was starting to make attempts to keep on floating. It was hard going, though, as the crud seemed to suck him down like quicksand. Practically his whole body was now caught in the sticky stuff.

"Watch out!" Harriet shouted.

Suddenly he felt something bubbling underneath his butt. And then he was flying, a powerful stream of water propelling him into the air. He flew up and away, and finally landed on the lawn, rain spraying him. Only it wasn't rain, as there wasn't a cloud in the sky. But water was still raining down on him. And then he saw what was going on: Harriet had opened the sprinklers, a part of which was installed in the rosebushes. She must have opened them all the way, for they'd propelled him right out of that puddle he was caught in.

He blinked as water soaked him. And then suddenly Harriet rose into his field of vision. She looked at him with such an expression of concern he didn't mind getting wet.

"Are you all right, snookums?" she asked, concern lacing her voice.

"I'm fine," he said. "You saved me."

"I realized something last night, snuggle pooh," she said softly.

"What's that?"

"That I love you too much to let this thing between us be over."

"Oh, Harriet," he said, a catch in his voice. "I've been such a fool. Can you ever forgive me?"

"I talked to Darlene. Last night in the park? She told me the truth. That you were a real gentlecat. And that you were never anywhere near her butt."

"She said that?"

"Not willingly. I may have mentioned slashing her throat."

He laughed. "Oh, honey muffin."

"Oh, love bug."

"You saved me!"

"That's something else I realized. Ever since we broke up you keep getting yourself into these dangerous situations. At this rate you're going to run out of your nine lives."

"I know. I think I'm at my sixth or my seventh."

"You need me, buttercup."

"I do need you."

"Without me you're going to fall from a cliff and there won't be a fat man to cushion your fall."

"Or I'll stumble into a duck pond and there won't be Chase to save me."

"Or you'll be swallowed up by a sinkhole and I won't be there to turn on the sprinklers."

They gazed softly into each other's eyes, and gently rubbed noses.

"It's almost like Jack and Rose on *Titanic*," Harriet giggled. "With all this water?"

"Only I have no intention of crawling off that raft," said Brutus.

"There was plenty of space on that raft for Jack!" Harriet cried.

"Right?"

They were quiet, and as Harriet lay down next to him, they both enjoyed this rare summer shower. And the pleasure of each other's company.

"A sinkhole," muttered Brutus. "In the rosebushes? How is that even possible?"

"I know, right?"

They gazed at each other. "I do need you, Harriet."

"And don't you ever forget it."

"I won't."

"Oh, sugar puff."

"Oh, cuppy cake."

"Oh, love angel."

"Oh, wuggle bear."

"Ugh," a voice softly pronounced nearby.

Brutus recognized it as Dooley's, and both he and Harriet laughed.

CHAPTER 34

*A*lec was so nice to take us to the hospital: Me and Dooley, and a waterlogged Brutus and Harriet, who, for some reason, had turned on the sprinklers in the backyard and had been enjoying a rain shower. At least they'd reconciled, and were suddenly all lovey-dovey again. So much so it was giving me a pain in the butt. Maybe that was the reason they fought in the first place, I suddenly realized: to enjoy that sweet reconciliation afterward.

"Now, I'm going to have to smuggle you into Odelia's room," Alec warned. "I don't think they like it when cats come to visit, so you guys will have to be extra-quiet, all right?"

"All right, Uncle Alec," we all sang in unison, even though he couldn't understand.

He smiled. "You guys are the best."

He'd arrived at the hospital and tucked us in two big, bulky plastic shopping bags. I hate being tucked into bags, but I was willing to make the sacrifice for Odelia's sake.

"What's going on with Harriet and Brutus?" I asked Dooley as we bumped up against each other while Uncle

166

Alec carried us into the hospital. The police chief was panting. Hard. Apparently four cats are a lot of weight to carry.

"I think they finally got over the whole Darlene thing," I said.

"Oh, so Harriet finally believes the perspective story?"

"It's not a story. There was a matter of perspective. I really believe Brutus's nose wasn't anywhere near Darlene's butt. Though from where I stood it definitely looked like it was."

"From where I was standing it looked as if his nose was up her tail," said Dooley, "but then my legs are shorter than yours."

"See? Brutus was right. It's all a matter of perspective."

This reminded me of the murder case Odelia and Chase had successfully solved. Ringo had claimed his master was right next to him when Dany was killed, but was he? Maybe he'd thought he was, but just like with Darlene, it was a matter of perspective.

But then we were set down on the floor, the bag was zipped open, and we hopped out of the bag and found ourselves in a hospital room. At least it smelled like one. Phew.

Uncle Alec picked me up first and deposited me on Odelia's bed, then did the same with the others. Odelia looked pale but alive, and she smiled weakly at the four of us.

"Hey, there, you guys. What happened, huh?"

"You conked your head on the bed," I said. "And scared the living crap out of us."

"I scared the living crap out of myself," she said.

I suddenly noticed we weren't alone in the room: Marge, Gran, Tex and Chase were all seated around Odelia's sickbed. Chase was staring at me intently, and I realized he probably figured this whole talking cats thing was really weird. Like, really, really weird.

"You better don't talk to Max too much, honey," said Marge. "You should rest."

"I'll rest when I'm dead," said Odelia, then realized her words could be interpreted as a little macabre, and corrected herself. "I'll sleep when you guys have left, I mean."

"The doctor is keeping her overnight," Marge explained for our sake. "He says she has a slight concussion."

"Nothing on the MRI, though," said Gran. "Which is a good thing," she added.

"Right," I said.

"I know what an MRI is," said Dooley. "I watch *General Hospital*, remember?"

"Of course you do," said Gran with a laugh.

They all laughed, except Tex and Chase and Alec, who weren't in on the joke.

"Dooley says he watches *General Hospital* all the time," Marge translated for the sake of the others. When Chase stared at her, she realized her mistake, and quickly shut up.

Too late, though, for Chase asked, "What's going on here?"

Marge said, a little uncertainly, "Oh, nothing. Just messing around. We like to pretend we can talk to our cats. Isn't that right, Mom?"

"Just a little game we play from time to time," said Gran. "And of course those little furballs are big talkers and talk right back at us—isn't that right, Maxie?"

She tickled my ear and I said, "I think you're in big trouble now, Gran."

"No, I'm not."

Chase was frowning, but didn't say anything.

"So what's all this about you guys being attacked by the man in the yellow parka?" asked Odelia, a little hoarsely.

"Not now, honey," said Marge. "You have to rest. In fact we should probably leave so you can get some more sleep."

"Don't leave. Just tell me what happened."

"A flowerpot was thrown at me," said Tex, his voice quaking with indignation. "Can you imagine? Someone actually tried to kill me with a flowerpot. I'm so upset right now."

"And I slipped on a roller skate," said Gran. "And I saw the guy who planted that skate. He was dressed in yellow—clearly the man in the yellow parka is working overtime."

"And a piece of the pirate ship almost dropped on me," said Marge.

"I checked the mast. It looks like it's been tampered with," said Uncle Alec gravely.

"So it's obvious, isn't it?" said Gran. "Someone is targeting this family, and they're doing everything they can to murder us and make it look like a string of accidents."

"Remember how they tried to run over Brutus?" Tex reminded the others.

"I don't know about this, you guys," said Odelia, her eyelids slowly closing. "It all seems far-fetched to me. Besides," she added, making an ultimate effort to open her eyes and look at her uncle Alec, "you have the man in the yellow parka locked up, haven't you?"

"I have," Alec confirmed.

"So the case is closed. End of story."

"He's still out there," Gran insisted. "And he's targeting us."

"Wolf Langdon has a mole on his hand," said Odelia, her eyes closing again. "Ringo says the man who killed Dany had a mole in the shape of an owl on his hand. Case... closed."

And so were her eyes. And this time she'd fallen asleep.

"Who is Ringo?" asked Chase in a low voice.

Uncle Alec waved his hand. "Just a witness who's come forward."

Chase looked taken aback. "What witness? I don't know

169

NIC SAINT

anything about a new witness, and I'm supposed to be in charge of this investigation."

Alec shrugged. "Ask Odelia."

Chase looked at Odelia and sighed. "Thank God her cats were home. I can't imagine her lying there all alone."

One by one, Odelia's family members got up and left the room, to allow her some peace and quiet. Knowing them, they'd all stay right there, not leaving her side until she was well enough to return home.

And the same went for me, Dooley, Brutus and Harriet.

Only we had the luxury of being able to sleep at the foot of her bed.

At least until the nurse came in and ushered us off the bed and onto a couch in the corner. "Cats don't belong in hospitals," she muttered darkly, but allowed us to stay anyway.

CHAPTER 35

n the hallway, Gran confronted Chase and her son. "I don't get it. You people are supposed to protect us. You're cops, for crying out loud. Your family is being targeted and you do nothing?"

"We've arrested the man in the yellow parka," said Alec, but he blinked under Gran's intense scrutiny.

"That just goes to show you arrested the wrong man. Cause the man in the yellow parka is still out there, and he's trying to kill us all. First Tex, then me and Marge. And it wouldn't surprise me if this man in the yellow parka didn't sneak into Odelia's room last night and planted that rug for her to slip on."

"That's ridiculous," said Alec.

"Odelia never trips and falls. And now she does? Just when the rest of this family is attacked? I don't think so." She poked a hole in Chase's chest. "And where were you when all this was going down, sonny boy?"

"I, um, was at the station interrogating Wolf Langdon, ma'am," said Chase. At least he didn't avert his eyes like Alec, who'd gone all weasely under Gran's furious glances.

"Well, you better interrogate him again, cause as far as I'm concerned, he's probably the leader of a gang of yellow parka men, operating all across town, and trying to get this family to die!"

She stalked off, feeling she'd said her piece and now it was up to the law enforcement people to do their jobs for a change.

Marge and Tex were seated in the waiting area, Marge nursing a cup of coffee, while Tex was checking something on his phone.

"My patients will need a replacement doctor while I'm in here," he explained when Gran sat down. "I've arranged for Dr. Rübler-Koss to take my place for the moment."

"Rübler-Koss? Isn't she specialized in palliative care?"

He shrugged. "She's a perfectly capable physician and she's stood in for me before." He placed the phone in his lap and rubbed his eyes. "Poor Odelia. I can't stop thinking about how if we'd been there half an hour later she might have suffered even worse."

"I just told off Alec and Chase. It doesn't do for them to twiddle their thumbs down at the police station while all of us are being hunted down by this bunch of maniacs!"

"Bunch of maniacs?" asked Marge. "You think there's more than one?"

"Of course! Just think, honey. He was in the house across the street when Tex was attacked with a highly lethal projectile."

"I wouldn't exactly call a flowerpot a lethal projectile," Tex protested.

"I would. Now shut up and listen to your mother-in-law for a change. Meanwhile, he was preparing a trap across the street. How is that possible? How can one man be in two places at the same time? Answer: he can't. Which means there's more than one attacker." She narrowed her eyes. "And the more I think about this, the more I'm convinced there's probably three or four, and that doesn't even include the ringleader, who's in prison right now. Though ringleader is probably a big word. If he allowed himself to be caught that easily, he's probably an amateur. The ringleader is probably the one who came for Odelia."

"It was a rug, Mom," said Marge. "Anyone can trip over a rug."

"Not Odelia," she said decidedly. "Odelia never trips over any rugs. No, that rug was definitely tampered with. So what we need is CSI. We need Gil Grissom and we need him now. Only Gil Grissom can figure out how they managed to tamper with that rug. Plus, Gil Grissom can probably lift fingerprints and DNA and whatnot from that rug, identifying the bastard who tried to kill our Odelia."

"I don't think even Gil Grissom could find fingerprints on an IKEA rug," said Tex, and Gran thought she detected a note of sarcasm in his voice.

She did not respond well to sarcasm, so she snapped, "Less lip from you, and more cooperation, Captain Underpants."

Tex frowned, and glanced down to where Gran was pointedly looking. Indeed: his underpants were showing just above the waistline of his beige slacks. "Must have snapped my belt when I jumped away from that flowerpot," he muttered, hoisting up his pants.

"Don't you think you're exaggerating, Mom?" asked Marge. "I'm not even sure a roller skate is a real murder weapon. Or a flowerpot for that matter."

"They are, and you better get with the program, missy. This gang uses everyday objects as murder weapons. They're like the MacGyver of killers. Besides, you just had a pirate boat drop on your head. Or do you think a sawn-off mast isn't a murder weapon either?"

She had Marge there. "Yes, that is odd," she admitted. "But who would do this? Who would target us?"

"I don't know but I'm going to find out," said Gran, darting nasty glances at Chase and Alec as they strolled into the waiting room. "Cause it's obvious to me that those two humpty dumpties would rather let us die than pull their heads out of their asses and lift a finger."

Just then, the doctor in charge of Odelia's recovery strode in. Dressed in his white coat, he looked particularly handsome, Gran thought. He was one of those hot young doctors you only see on medical shows, and she instantly took a shine to him. Though she knew from experience handsome young doctors were all hiding secrets. Like an evil twin. Or a fraudulent degree from a fake university. Or even a third nipple in a really weird place.

"Good news," said the handsome young doctor as he addressed his audience. "Odelia will make a full recovery. We found nothing alarming on the MRI scan and there's no swelling of the brain, no contusion, nothing to indicate any lasting damage. I would like to keep her overnight just to make sure, but apart from that, I'm positive she'll be just fine."

"Oh, thank God," said Marge, bringing her hands to her face. Tears were falling like dewy rain, and Gran didn't wonder. She herself had experienced a twinge of dread when she saw her beloved granddaughter in such a terrible state.

"She was lucky," the doctor acknowledged. "If she'd fallen even one centimeter to the left or to right, things could have been a lot worse." He turned to Uncle Alec. "Odelia told me this was an accident?"

"It was," said Alec, giving Gran a look of defiance.

"It wasn't," Gran instantly shot back. "My granddaughter was attacked in her own home by the notorious Yellow Parka MacGyver Gang, and the members of this gang have yet to be caught. All the while, the police are doing nothing to stop the carnage. Nothing!"

The handsome young doctor frowned. "That's very disturbing. I hope you catch this... Yellow Parka MacGyver Gang before they cause more harm."

Alec pressed his lips together. He clearly wasn't happy with Gran's intervention.

"Oh, don't worry," said Gran. She tapped her chest. "*I'll* catch them. Because when the people paid to protect the citizens of this community fail to do their job, it's up to us to take matters into our own hands and go after the bastards ourselves."

The doctor gave her a puzzled look, then nodded. "Well, then. I'll keep you all informed of Odelia's progress. In the meantime, you can join her again. But don't keep her up. What she needs right now is rest, rest, and more rest."

And with these words, he was off at a brisk trot.

"What are you up to, Ma?" asked Alec, a note of ice in his voice.

"I'm going to catch the bastards, just like I said. Cause if they tried to kill her once, they'll try again—and I promise you I'll be there when they do, and I'll strike them down with my fist of fury!" She shook her bony fist to emphasize her words and walked off.

CHAPTER 36

*A*lec and Chase stood conferring by the vending machine. Alec was nursing a styrofoam cup of watery coffee, wondering why the brew in these places always tasted like sewage.

"What do you make of Vesta's wild accusations?" Chase asked.

Alec shook his head. "You know what my mother is like." He just hoped she wouldn't go out and start some kind of private vigilante search for this gang of men in yellow parkas.

"Yeah, but she's not completely unhinged. There are signs that something is seriously wrong here. Like that mast dropping on Marge. That was tampered with, right?"

Alec heaved a deep sigh. "I know that's what I said but now I'm not so sure."

"What do you mean you're not so sure?"

"At first glance, I'd say that yes, someone sawed through that thing, but now that I think about it, it could have simply been shoddy construction. An expert will have to determine what caused that mast to collapse when it did."

"And what about Tex and his flowerpot incident?"

"Coincidence," said Alec. "We searched that house top to bottom. No indication anyone was even in there when that flowerpot fell down. I'm blaming it on a draft that kicked open a window and knocked down that pot. Like I said, just a coincidence."

"And the roller skate? Or Odelia's rug?"

"Accidents. Anyone could trip over a roller skate, or a rug. How would an attacker even know Vesta would be the one to walk by at that exact moment, and step on that exact skate? Unless he was psychic, which I think we can agree is just crazy talk. Nah. That skate was left by some kid, and Vesta just happened to trip over it. Same thing with Odelia's rug."

"What about Brutus almost being run over?"

"Same thing. Cats get run over by careless drivers every single day. Why would this be any different? The only thing that makes this a strange case is the fact that all these accidents happened within the space of a day, to members of the same family. That is weird. But not criminal."

Chase nodded. "I'm glad you say so cause I think you're absolutely right. Only thing worrying me is Vesta going off like a loose cannon, stirring up trouble all over the place."

Alec wholeheartedly agreed with his younger colleague. Then again, Vesta would do what Vesta would do. Not a damn thing they could do about it. "All in all I'm pretty satisfied only one crime was committed here. And that's Dany Cooper's murder."

"And we have her killer in custody, so case closed."

"Case closed," Alec agreed. The comment about the mole had been the final piece of the puzzle. Now he was fully convinced Wolf Langdon was the man they'd been looking for.

"Then I only have one question for you," said Chase as he

took a sip from his own cup and winced, then dumped it in the trash.

"Yeah?"

"Who is Ringo?"

Uh-oh. "Um... Ringo?"

"The witness you mentioned? You said a new witness came forward and he testified that Dany's murderer had an owl-shaped mole on the back of his right hand?"

"Yeah, that wasn't a witness, per se," he said, backtracking.

"So what is he? And can I talk to this Ringo character?"

"Ringo is, um, not someone who reached out to us," said Alec carefully. "He actually came to Odelia. He's one of her sources. And you know how Odelia is about her sources."

Chase groaned. "Not again. What is it with Odelia and her mysterious sources?"

"Reporters, Chase. That's how they operate."

"So when can I have a crack at this Ringo?"

"You'll have to ask Odelia. But I think you already know the answer."

"Dammit. I wanted to have a chat with this Ringo. Tie up the case with a neat bow."

Alec suppressed a smile. Tough to have a chat with a Chihuahua.

Though Ringo would probably love the bow.

CHAPTER 37

*T*ex and Marge were the only ones left in the small hospital waiting room. And they weren't going anywhere. Even though the doctor had said there was nothing they could do there, and Odelia slept peacefully, Marge couldn't imagine going home, or going to work, while her little girl was laid up in her room. She would have preferred to sit by her side, but after the doctor had left, a nurse had told them it would be a little while before they could go back in there, as they needed to run some tests and take care of some other stuff.

"I don't get it," she said, rubbing her arms. "What tests? What stuff? Odelia is sleeping, the doctor told us so himself. What can they possibly be doing to my baby?"

"I'm sure they know what they're doing," said Tex, taking her hand and patting it consolingly.

"You're a doctor, Tex. Can't you ask them what's going on?"

"You heard what's going on. They're running some tests and they'll let us know when we can get in there."

"But what tests?!"

She knew she was acting like a hysteric but frankly she didn't care. Her only daughter had almost died today and she wasn't going to be calm and rational for quite some time while she tried to deal with this emergency. She didn't even care anymore that she'd only escaped death by inches herself, and so had Tex and even Vesta.

"What's going on, Tex? Do you really think there's a gang out there trying to kill us?"

"Alec doesn't seem to think so," Tex said carefully.

"But my mother does, and look how often she's been proved right."

"And how often she's been proved wrong," said Tex, still patting her hand.

She jerked it from his grasp. "I don't understand. Something is happening and it scares me."

"Everything will be just fine," said Tex, though he didn't sound convinced himself. He looked up at the nurse, but she merely passed by, without a message to share this time. "And I'm sure they know perfectly well what they're doing," he added.

Marge bit her lower lip. If she kept this up she wouldn't have a lip left by the time Odelia was allowed to go home. "Remember how beautiful she was?"

Tex immediately knew what she was talking about, for he smiled. "She still is."

"She is, isn't she? Our beautiful darling baby girl. Oh, Tex. I don't know what I'd do if something happened to her."

"Nothing is going to happen to her. She has her guardian angels looking out for her."

"Do you think that if Max and Dooley hadn't been there, she would have taken an even nastier fall?"

"I'm sure of it. Somehow—and I don't know how any of this works—this gift you and Odelia share—and Vesta," he added grudgingly, "not only gives you the power to communicate with cats, it also seems to have transferred to you certain qualities cats have. Amongst them the whole nine lives thing."

"You don't think that's just a myth?"

"No, actually I don't. Cats are notoriously hard to kill, and so are you and Odelia."

"And Mom."

"And your mom," he said reluctantly.

Marge smiled. "You don't really believe we have nine lives, do you?"

"Why not? You can talk to those sweethearts, why not share other traits as well?"

It definitely was a comforting thought.

"Do you think Chase knows?" she asked.

"Knows what? That you can talk to cats? I don't think so."

"I forgot he was there for a moment. In Odelia's room? He was giving me some very strange looks."

"We can simply ascribe that to your general state of mind. You were very distraught, honey. We all were."

"True, but maybe it's time we told him? I told you at a certain point, remember?"

Tex smiled at the memory. "I didn't believe you at first. I thought you were pulling my leg."

"Chase will, too. But we still owe it to him to know the truth about this family. Especially if…"

"He and Odelia end up together."

"Which I'm starting to think they will."

"I think so, too. He seems really smitten with her."

"And she with him."

She was feeling calmer now. Talking things through with her husband always had that effect on her. She looked up into his face. "You know? You're the best thing that ever happened to me, Tex. And I don't say this nearly often enough."

"You're the best thing that ever happened to me, too, Marge," he said.

They kissed, and didn't even hear it when the nurse walked up to them, on those rubber-soled nurse's sneakers of hers. But when she cleared her throat, and said, "You can go in now," Marge's heart jumped. Maybe Tex was right, and things would be just fine.

After all, weren't they always?

CHAPTER 38

There was a knock at the door of Odelia's room and a man poked his head in. He wasn't a doctor or a nurse but still seemed vaguely familiar to me. When he saw that the couch was covered in cats, he smiled. Immediately I warmed to him. I can never dislike a cat person, and this man obviously was one.

Odelia opened her eyes and stared at the man for a moment, then also smiled. "Conway. How did you know I was here?"

"A member of the crew heard you had an accident, so I made it my mission to find out which hospital you'd been taken to."

"That's very sweet of you."

He strode further into the room, and spirited a large bouquet of flowers from behind his back and offered it to Odelia. She was almost hidden behind the huge selection of blooms.

"They're lovely," she said, taking a sniff. "You shouldn't have."

"They're from the entire crew, wishing you a speedy recovery."

He took a seat next to the bed, then a tentative peek at the bandages that covered the right part of Odelia's head. "So how are you feeling?"

"Oh, it looks a lot worse than it is," she assured him. "Just me being clumsy, I guess. Tripped over a carpet, if you can believe it. Silly me."

"Could happen to anyone," he said. "In fact it happened to me once. I broke an arm in the process."

"In that case I guess I was lucky." She waved her arms. "No broken bones."

He laughed and settled back in his chair, which creaked. "I have a proposal for you, Odelia."

"Oh, not a wedding proposal, I hope. I'm afraid I'm taken already."

He laughed again, throwing his head back.

He looked like a nice person, I thought. He had one of those rolled-out-of-bed hairdos and a three-day beard that made him look what most women would consider extremely sexy. He was dressed in a black leather jacket, skinny jeans, and cowboy boots. The ultimate bad boy. I wondered if he was an actor, too.

"No, nothing like that, I'm afraid," he said. "The thing is, we're going to continue the Hampton Cove Bard in the Park shows. We're actually going through with it. We had a big meeting this morning at the manor and it was decided we don't want to give this up. Even Don agreed, if you can believe it. Though he demanded a bigger part for himself, of course."

"Of course. So you found another director."

"We have. I don't think you know her. Vita Bogdanovich. She's very good. Not like Wolf, of course, but she's one of the best at what she does. The thing is, Emily and I have been thinking things through. What with Wolf being in jail and all, and in light of the terrible things he's done, we're going to rename the company, and do some restructuring. We're also going to have to reconsider our production slate, and now I'm finally getting to the point," he said when Odelia yawned.

"Don't mind me. It's the stuff they put in my drip. It just makes me woozy."

What made Odelia woozy was probably the slight concussion she'd suffered, I thought, but my own eyes were also drooping closed. The hospital room was nice and warm, and the couch soft and comfy.

"The thing is, we're staging a production of Mary Poppins in the spring, and Wolf had been looking for someone to play Mary. He'd mentioned a couple of times how he thought Dany Cooper was perfect for the part. So now with Dany gone—and Wolf…" He looked at Odelia expectantly. "I was hoping that you'd be interested."

"You want me to help you find your Mary Poppins?"

"As far as I'm concerned, we've found her already, and with your permission I'd like to make it official. I talked to Emily, and showed her some of your footage, and she agrees."

Odelia frowned. "With my permission? Why do you need my permission?"

"Because you're she. You're our Mary Poppins. Only if you want, of course."

Odelia let out a little squeak of delight. "Me? You want me to play Mary?"

He was grinning widely. "Yes, we do. We can't think of a better person to embody the spirit of Mary, and from what we've seen you're born to play the part. A natural."

Odelia didn't know what to say, that much was obvious. Her mouth opened and closed a few times, but her eyes were sparkling, which probably meant she liked the idea.

"Who's Mary Poppins?" asked Dooley, who'd been listening intently.

"She's a governess who can fly and do all kinds of magic," I said. "Don't you remember? We saw the movie just the other day. The one with Emily Blunt."

"Fly? A governess who can fly?"

"She's from England," I said, and he nodded, as if that explained everything.

Brutus yawned. "So Odelia is going to be an actress. Cool. I just hope she won't have to travel the world. I hate to travel."

"And who says she'll take us along on her travels?" said Harriet. "I know for a fact that actors never take their cats along with them. Shanille's human has a sister whose second cousin twice removed is an actress and when she flies out for some movie she's shooting up in Canada or wherever, she always asks Father Reilly's sister to take care of her cats for her."

"She's not going to take us along with her?" asked Dooley. "But that's just wrong."

"Cats don't travel," said Harriet decidedly. "Everybody knows that. Dogs do, which is why many people who travel a lot prefer to get a dog and dump their cats at the pound."

"I travel," I said. "I would love to travel with Odelia."

Frankly, I wouldn't. I like my home, I like my couch, I like my backyard, I like my friends and I like my routine. Traveling simply seems like a terrible way to occupy your time, not to mention having to sleep in strange beds, and meet a lot of strange people. If Odelia insisted, I'd do it in a heartbeat, of course. But after Harriet's words I was starting to think she wouldn't insist.

"So what do you say?" asked this Conway person. "Say yes," he added with a twinkle in his eye.

I had to hand it to him. He was very charming, apart from being very handsome.

"I'll have to think about it," said Odelia. "And discuss it with my boyfriend, not to mention my boss."

"Your boss? Oh, right. The reporter thing." He seemed to figure that wasn't a big deal. "You can take a leave of absence, though, can't you?"

"I'm Dan's only reporter," Odelia explained. "If I take a leave of absence he'll have to hire another reporter, and there aren't that many reporters in Hampton Cove."

She was the only one, I knew. Reporters don't grow on trees in small towns like Hampton Cove. It was a miracle Dan had found Odelia. If not for her he'd probably have had to close down the Gazette when he decided to retire. Now she was poised to take over when he did.

Conway seemed displeased for some reason. "This is a once-in-a-lifetime opportunity, Odelia."

"I know it is. And I'm very excited. But I'll still need time to think."

He frowned, clearly not used to being turned down like this.

"Have it your way," he said a little grumpily. "I thought you'd jump at the chance, but clearly I was mistaken."

"Oh, but I think it's a wonderful opportunity. It's just…"

He silenced her with an imperious gesture. "Don't think too long. This offer is time-sensitive."

It sounded a lot like a threat, and suddenly I liked handsome dude a lot less.

Being the diplomat she was, Odelia decided to change the subject. "So have you visited Wolf in prison?"

"No, I haven't," he said. "I don't know what I'll say to him when I do. He's just…" He raked his fingers through his shaggy mane. "He's one of my oldest friends. I just can't believe he'd do a thing like that."

"I know," she said. "He never struck me as the murderous type. Then again, you just never know, do you?"

"No, I guess you don't. Is it true that you're the one who caught him?"

She nodded. "Me and Chase—that's my boyfriend. He's a local detective."

"Oh, I've seen him. Talked to him, even."

"That's right. Chase interviewed everyone."

"He was very thorough." Conway frowned. "Just tell me one thing. Simply to satisfy my personal curiosity. The papers never mention stuff like that. How did you know it was him?"

"A witness came forward. She said the killer was wearing a yellow jacket—a yellow parka, as a matter of fact. And then we found a yellow parka hanging in Wolf's closet. It still had Dany's blood on it."

"Terrible," said Conway, shaking his head. "That's just terrible."

"Also, another witness said the killer had an owl-shaped mole on the back of his right hand, and Wolf has just such a mole."

"A witness said that?" Conway seemed surprised by this.

Odelia nodded. "She saw the killer and even though she didn't get a good look at his face, she did see his hand."

"So this second witness is a she, huh? And will she testify in court?"

Odelia cast a quick glance in my direction, and I shook my head. No, Rita would definitely not testify in court, that much was obvious, and neither would Ringo.

"You'll have to ask my uncle," she said, still the diplomat. "He's the chief of police."

"Right." He flashed her a quick smile. "You're something of a sleuthhound, aren't you, Odelia?"

"Reporter, sleuth—this girl wears many hats, Con."

"She does. And now she's going to be a star on the stage, too."

His phone jangled in his pocket and he took it out. And as he answered it, I saw Odelia stare at the man, her eyes suddenly wide, and her face almost as white as the sheets she was lying under.

But then Conway excused himself, got up and walked out just when Tex and Marge walked in.

Odelia stared at me, then said slowly, "The owl-shaped mole."

"What about it?" I said.

"Conway has one. On his right hand."

CHAPTER 39

Odelia had called an emergency meeting, and it was being held in her hospital room. Not the best place in the world to hold a meeting, but she had no other choice. The doctor advised against her discharging herself from the hospital, and so did her dad. And she wasn't going to put herself in danger by going against their wishes.

Around her sat her mom and dad, her uncle Alec, and Chase, of course. They'd tried to locate Gran but hadn't succeeded. She was off somewhere on a quest to locate the Yellow Parka MacGyver Gang and wasn't answering her phone.

"So what's so important?" asked Uncle Alec.

"It's about your head, isn't it?" said Marge. "The doctor has found a tumor!"

"No, nothing like that," Odelia was quick to put her mother's mind at ease. "This isn't about me. It's about Dany Cooper."

"Dany? You've uncovered some more information?" asked Chase.

"I have. You locked up the wrong man. Wolf Langdon didn't kill Dany."

There were gasps of shock around her hospital bed. In a corner of the room, four cats also stirred. The nurses, understanding Odelia wasn't going to part with her cats, even though they didn't agree, had brought in blankets, bowls of food and water, and even a litter box. It was an unusual arrangement, but Tex had talked to the head nurse, and had convinced her it would help Odelia enormously in her recovery, and she'd grudgingly agreed.

"How do you know?" asked Chase, reluctant to let go of his main suspect.

"Remember how I mentioned Ringo?"

"The mysterious witness," said Chase, shuffling uncomfortably in his chair.

"Ringo said he saw the murder, and led me to a second witness. Her name is Rita. And she said the thing that made the killer stand out was an owl-shaped mole on the back of his hand. I checked pictures of Wolf's right hand. He has a mole, but it's not owl-shaped."

She held up her phone, and showed a close-up of Wolf's mole to the others.

"It's more, like, pear-shaped," Marge said.

"Pear-shaped, owl-shaped. Who cares?" said Chase. "The guy did it. He had the parka still hanging in his closet. You saw it yourself!"

"That's what I thought, until a man came to visit me earlier, and he does have an owl-shaped mole on his hand. Conway Kemp."

"Wolf's business partner? Why would he kill Dany?"

"I've talked to several crew members this afternoon—I have nothing better to do while I'm laid up here anyway."

"Honey, you're supposed to rest, not conduct a murder investigation over the phone," said her dad.

"I know, but an innocent man is in jail, and the real killer is walking around a free man. What do you expect me to do? Besides, I feel fine," she added waving away her dad's tut-tutting. "The thing is, Conway was madly in love with Dany."

"How do you know?" asked Chase, who was proving hardest to convince.

"Several people said he'd been making advances towards her ever since production started. He's the one who discovered her, not Wolf. And apparently Con had this crazy idea of taking her to the top as her husband-manager. She fell for Wolf, though, and wasn't interested in Con. He kept showering her with gifts, though, and asking her out, and she kept turning him down. I think he must have lost it yesterday, after she turned him down yet again. He stabbed her in a fit of rage and left the yellow parka in Wolf's closet to frame him."

"But we found that parka by accident. Nobody told us where to find it," said Chase.

"I'm pretty sure Con would have put in an anonymous call to put us onto the parka. Only we beat him to it, which made things work out even better than he'd expected."

"This is all conjecture," Chase pointed out. "For one thing, who are these witnesses? This Ringo and this Rita? Are you going to produce them so they can testify in court?"

"We need to extract a confession from Conway Kemp," said Uncle Alec.

"We'd have to arrest him first. And on what grounds? The word of two witnesses who won't come forward? A mole on his hand?" Chase shook his head. "This is ridiculous. Odelia, honey, I've gone along with this as far as I can, but you're just grasping at straws."

"I'm not crazy, Chase. Conway killed Dany. I just know he did," she said.

Chase was looking at her as if this bump on her head had messed with her sanity, and she hated it.

"I'm not going to arrest a man based on some flimsy 'evidence,'" said Chase. "We have a solid case against Langdon and I'm sure the judge will agree with me on that. How about you, Chief?"

Uncle Alec was in a tough spot. Either he sided with his niece, on the basis of evidence he would never be able to bring into court, or he sided with his lead detective, knowing he was dead wrong. Either way, he would be criticized.

"I think—" he began.

But he was interrupted by some type of loud commotion outside.

He got up, and so did the others, and moved over to the window.

Underneath Odelia's window, on the hospital parking lot, Gran was holding up a sign that read, 'Justice for the Pooles. Arrest the Yellow Parka Gang Now!'

"End police incompetence!" she yelled when she caught sight of her son. "Put our tax dollars to work now!"

CHAPTER 40

*C*onway Kemp was in a lousy mood. He'd offered the part of Mary Poppins to that Odelia Poole and she still hadn't gotten back to him. He didn't get it. Any other actor would have jumped at the chance to accept a plum part like that, potentially launching her career, and this woman preferred to stay buried in this small town and work as a stupid reporter?

Women. One was even dumber than the next.

It was late already, and he passed by the dining room on his way to the small theater Marcia Graydon had installed in the basement. He'd gotten a text from Marisa, one of the interns helping out in the script department, to meet him down in the theater. She had something urgent she needed to discuss with him that couldn't wait.

He hated stuff like that, but it all came with the territory. When you were a producer on any project, you tried to take care of the small stuff, unburdening the creatives as much as you could. Hiring people was part of the process, and so was keeping them happy and productive.

So even though he wanted to hit the hay and zonk out, he

crossed the dining room and then the few steps down into the basement. A small stage had been erected there, with a large pull-down projector screen, so the 100-seat theater could double as a private screening room.

They'd been using the theater for rehearsals and script readings, before they went out and rehearsed at the park, where the production would eventually be staged once all the pieces were in place. Until then, the theater was the creative hub of the project.

"Marisa?" he called out when he entered. The lights were doused, but there was one lone bulb lit on stage. Weird. And a little creepy. "Marisa? You wanted to talk to me?"

He crossed the room and mounted the stage, wondering where the damn girl could be. Would be typical, of course, for her to have some imagined or real emergency, only to completely forget about it a minute later.

Probably boyfriend trouble. Being away from home, and staying with a bunch of other young people at a fancy mansion in the Hamptons, things tended to get a little out of control. Add to that the stacks of weed these kids consumed, and it was a miracle Bard in the Park didn't turn full-on Woodstock. It was the kind of stuff Con had to deal with on a daily basis. Sometimes he wondered if he shouldn't have stayed in the Marines. He sometimes hated these so-called creatives. Bunch of nutcases, every last one of them.

He was surprised to find a bunch of cats seated on stage. Weird. Wherever he turned these days, he seemed to encounter cats. They were staring at him, unmoving, those eyes unblinking and frankly more than a little scary, the single bulb reflected in those dark orbs.

He had never admitted it to anyone, but he hated cats. They gave him the creeps. The way they could just stare at you, as if looking straight into your soul. Brrrr.

"Marisa!" He yelled. "Where the hell are you?"

Suddenly, from the wings, a figure stepped forward. He gulped when he recognized her as... Dany Cooper! She even had the knife still stuck in her chest, blood oozing from the wound, as well as from her lips, and when she spoke, it was with a haunting undertone.

"Why did you do it, Con? Why did you kill me? I thought you loved me?"

"I—what—this isn't happening," he stammered, staggering back. "What's going on?"

"Oh, I'm real, Con. As real as you. I can't seem to find peace. Not until I know why you did it. Why, Con? Why did you kill me? I liked you. I know you liked me. You kept saying it all the time. And sending me those gifts. Those expensive perfumes, clothes, underwear…"

"I did like you—I mean I still do—I… Oh, God!" A creature suddenly scurried through his legs and he yelped, then fell to the floor. He watched with dread as Dany approached.

He couldn't help but notice how pale her face was—so horribly pale, all the blood having drained from it and out of that wound.

On the floor there was a steady drip-drip-drip of blood as she walked.

"Why, Con?" she repeated. "Can't you see? I need to know. Why did you kill me? I still had so much to live for. So much talent. So much life. Wasted. Because of you."

"I didn't—I don't…"

"I was so young. And you killed me. You destroyed me. You're responsible…"

"It's your own damn fault!" he screamed as another cat scurried past him, then hissed, and moved on. This wasn't happening! Was he going crazy? He must be. Ghosts didn't exist, did they? But Dany seemed awfully real. There was even some dirt caked to her hair, and the side of her face. Even her clothes, the same clothes she was wearing when she died, were streaked with mud. She'd dragged herself here straight from the grave!

"Why did you kill me, Con?" she said, repeating the same mantra, as she drew inexorably closer to him, still that steady drip-drip-drip of blood. Thick, dark liquid oozing out of her, now flowing from her mouth—out of the corners of her eyes —her nose—her ears!

"Stop! Don't you come near me!" he yelled, crawling back towards the edge of the stage. "You brought this on yourself. You didn't want me. I asked you again and again. I would have given you everything. Not like Wolf. That loser would never have left his wife for you. Never! He couldn't. She was his lifeline. His financial backbone. Without his wife, he was nothing, and the company was nothing. I told you, but you wouldn't believe me. You kept hoping he would leave his wife but I told you—he wasn't going to do that.

"Oh, why did you throw yourself away on that loser?" he lamented. "Why? And then when I told you, you just laughed. You laughed! I declared my everlasting love and you threw it back in my face! So I lost it. I had the knife in my hand from peeling an apple so I stabbed you. I never meant to hurt you. How could I! I love you, Dany. I love you! Oh, I'm so sorry…"

He collapsed into a blubbering mess of mucus and misery. She was upon him, bending over him, dripping her blood on him. He felt it. In his hair. Then she reached out a hand and touched him and he screamed!

"No—don't take me with you!" he yelled. "I'm sorry! I'm so sorry!"

"And you should be," Dany said. Only her voice had suddenly taken on a different timbre.

And as he looked up into her face, she smiled. He blinked. "What's going on?"

From across the stage, several people now came walking out. He recognized Marisa, the intern who'd texted him, and

Bernice from makeup, Janice from the costume department, but also that police chief, and Detective Kingsley.

"Conway Kemp," said the Chief sternly. "You're under arrest for the murder of Dany Cooper."

He snapped his head up, to take in Dany again. "Dany? What's going on?"

"I'm not Dany, Con," said the woman, as she accepted a paper towel from Bernice and started wiping away her makeup. "But if I were, I'd tell you that you're a monster. And that you'll be punished for what you did to her."

And only then did he recognize her as Odelia Poole.

Oh, darn it.

CHAPTER 41

*O*ur humans were all seated around the table in Marge's backyard. Tex was incinerating burger patties on the grill, with the expert assistance of Alec and Chase, while Gran was listening intently to Odelia and Marge trying to make a few things clear about this case.

"So there never was a yellow parka gang?" the old lady asked, looking confused.

"No, there wasn't. Those were all random accidents that just happened to happen on the same day," Marge explained

"But the mast of the pirate ship? That was tampered with, right?"

"Construction error. That mast could have dropped down any time. Someone had glued those two pieces together instead of using bolts. The glue didn't hold and the whole thing came crashing down."

"But I saw a man dressed in yellow," Gran insisted.

"Probably the person who lives in that house, wearing a yellow sweater," said Odelia.

"What about you, Tex?" Gran bellowed over the sound of

the sizzling burgers. "You saw a man shove that flowerpot from the windowsill, didn't you?"

"Quite frankly I never saw anyone," said Tex, a little sheepish. "I saw movement, but that was probably just the window flapping, which was the reason the pot dropped down in the first place."

"I don't get it," said Gran, shaking her head in frustration. "I was so sure there was a gang targeting us."

"No gang. Just a bunch of freak accidents," said Odelia.

"But stuff like that never happened to us before!" Gran insisted. "So why did it happen now?"

Odelia nor Marge had an answer to that.

"I think I know what happened," said Dooley.

We were all seated on the porch swing, and we stared at Dooley.

"Why is that?" asked Harriet.

"Because the universe wanted to demonstrate just how well-protected the Pooles are. And what better way to do that than by engaging them in a series of near-fatal accidents?"

Those were some real words of wisdom, and coming from Dooley, too!

"Sounds plausible," I said. "If you accept that there is a universe that's wise and conscious."

"Of course there is," said Dooley. "Why else would it have placed us in this family, with such nice people? That can't be a coincidence, can it?"

It was a tough proposition to ponder, and my head was already hurting.

"I don't know about all of that," said Brutus. "I'm just glad I ended up where I am." He gave Harriet a tiny nudge, and she giggled.

"So am I," she said.

The two love birds quickly tired of our company, and

hopped off the porch to celebrate their newfound reconciliation in their favored rosebushes. The sinkhole had been filled up by Gran, and the bushes had been made cat-safe once more.

"There's one thing that still puzzles me, though," said Dooley.

"What's that?"

"Why weren't there any fingerprints on the knife Conway used to kill Dany?"

That was a question I could answer. "He wiped them off. Before *he* took off."

"So it was a crime of passion?"

"It was. He didn't plan to kill her. It just happened. And he couldn't believe his luck that no one had seen him."

"So why did he try to frame Wolf? Wasn't he supposed to be his best friend?"

"He secretly hated Wolf for seducing Dany and playing fast and loose with her."

"He did it all for love," said Dooley with a sigh.

"He did it because he couldn't accept that when a woman says No, she means No."

Just then, Chase sat down on the porch next to us, leaned his arms on the back support and glanced the other way. "So what's all this about a witness named Ringo, huh?"

He glanced in our direction, as we stared back at him, dubious.

"Do you think he understands us now?" asked Dooley.

"I'm not sure. Tell him something."

"Hello, Chase!" Dooley said with emphasis. "Do you understand what I'm saying?"

Chase laughed. "I must be going crazy. Talking to a bunch of cats."

"I don't think he can understand us," I said.

"No, I don't think so either."

"Oh, God," said Chase, glancing up at the sky. "You know? I don't know about you guys, but there's something really funny going on with this family. The way all the women keep chatting with their cats, as if they can actually understand a word they're saying. And how Odelia keeps dragging mysterious witnesses from her hat." He shook his head. "If I put my detective's cap on, I'd say she does actually... talk to you guys. Which, as we all know, is impossible." He glanced over to us. This time we just stared at him, without uttering a word.

Was Chase onto Odelia's secret? That wasn't good. Or was it?

Chase laughed. "See? I'm doing it again. Talking to a bunch of dumb animals. Let me just make one thing perfectly clear." He leaned in, and lowered his voice. "This family may be weird, but I love the hell out of them. All of them—even Odelia's pain-in-the-ass Granny. And I know that you do, too. So let's make a deal, all right? I'm going to promise to take good care of you guys, if you promise to take good care of Odelia. Deal?"

"Deal," both Dooley and I said in unison.

I'd always liked Chase, and now I was liking him even more, if possible.

Chase stared at us. "Well, I'll be damned," he muttered. "You little dudes *can* talk."

"Of course we can talk," said Dooley. "What do you take us for? Dumb animals?"

"That's exactly what he takes us for, Dooley," I said. "He just said so."

"I know, but he was probably kidding, right? Weren't you kidding, Chase?"

But the cop was shaking his head. "Holy crap. This is some weird shit right there."

"I resent being called weird shit," I told him.

I liked Odelia's boyfriend, but not if he was going to start calling us names.

"Okay. Let's try this again," he said. "Max."

"Yes, Chase?"

"Can you understand me?"

"Of course I can understand you. Now ask me a real question."

"Holy mackerel. You cats can hear me! And talk back at me!"

I gulped and turned to Dooley. "Did we just reveal Odelia's big secret?"

"I think we did," said Dooley, looking equally stricken.

Chase then pressed his index finger to his lips. "Let's keep this between us for now, you guys." He then got up, and muttered, "Holy moly. This is big. This is, like, huge."

Holy moly was right, and so was huge. Huge trouble. For us!

Chapter One

"Scott! Get up! Time for breakfast!"

Scott groaned, opened one eye and saw that the day had already started without him. He didn't mind. As far as he was concerned, the day could do whatever it wanted. So he closed his eyes again and tried to return to the dream he'd abandoned. The one where he was Han Solo and instead of having to endure that weird hairy ape as a traveling companion he conquered the universe with Emilia Clarke by his side. Now wouldn't *that* be something!

But before he and lovely Emilia could board the Millennium Falcon, Mom's voice pierced the fragile fabric of sleep once more—effectively ending his roseate dreamscape.

"Scott! Out of bed! Now!"

He threw back the comforter, rubbed the sleep from his eyes and yawned. Checking his smartphone, he saw that his best friend Mike was still asleep. If he wasn't he'd have sent him an update on his Pokemon Go conquests from last night. They might be twelve, but that didn't mean Pokemon was beneath them now. Besides, with the new Harry Potter Pokemon coming out soon, they needed to work on their mad skillz.

Shuffling out of his room in the direction of the bathroom, he discovered the door locked. Dragging one hand through his shaggy mane, he pounded the door with the other.

"Go away, scuzz-ball!" his sister yelled from inside.

"You go away, snarf-face!" he yelled back.

"Don't call your sister a snarf-face," said his mother as she hurried past, cradling the baby in her arms.

"Why do you keep carrying Jacob everywhere?" he asked. "He's old enough to walk."

But Mom wasn't listening. Instead, she was pounding down the stairs, still carrying Jacob as if his legs were too weak to carry him. At this rate, the toddler was never going to learn how to walk all by himself. Scott shook his head. Adults. They just never listened.

The door to the bathroom suddenly swung open and Maya appeared, a towel draped around her head and another one around her bony frame. She narrowed her eyes at him. "Why do you need the bathroom anyway? You wear the same grungy shirt three days in a row and you don't even bother to deodorize those pathetic pits of yours."

"I don't need to deodorize my pits," he said, moving past his sister. "My pits naturally smell like roses."

"Nobody's pits smell like roses. Especially yours, little brother."

He squared off against Maya. Even though she was five years older than him, they were the same height. He'd gotten a growth spurt last year to the extent she had no right to call him 'little brother' anymore. "Are you dissing my pits?"

"I'm telling you that if you don't start working on your

personal hygiene no girl is ever going to want to go out with you."

He laughed at this. "Who cares about girls?! All girls are stupid!"

"Have it your own way, freak. I'm just trying to look out for you."

She stomped off, and he plodded into the bathroom and slammed the door.

Dee heard the door slam and yelled, "Don't slam the door!"

Not that it would do much good. Her kids were at the stage where they'd stopped listening to anything she or Tom said. She remembered just in time not to frown. She was turning forty next year, and she could almost feel the collagen in her face breaking down as that fateful birthday drew closer. Likewise, she tried not to smile too much either, or pucker her lips. She darted a quick look in the hallway mirror. The woman who looked back at her was fair-haired, light-skinned, and quite beautiful. She also had dark rings under her eyes that hadn't been there when she was her lookalike daughter's age. Ugh.

Inadvertently, she'd put Jacob down. The toddler was looking up at her, then gave her a cheerful smile. "Mommy!" he cried, then held out his arms. "Carry!"

Scott's words hadn't missed their effect, though. Her son was right. The days of lugging the little tyke all over the place were over. In Dee's defense, though, she only carried him up and down the stairs these days, and only when she was in a hurry. "Go to the kitchen," she said encouragingly. "Go and find Daddy."

"Daddy!" Jacob said, and lo and behold, he moved off at an awkward wobble in the general direction of the kitchen.

As she followed him at a little distance, Dee smiled. He was such a lively, cheerful little dude. Never gave his mom and dad any trouble at all. Unlike Scott, who'd been a real cryer, and Maya, who'd been a restless kid. Looked like third time was the charm after all.

Behind her, Ralph came trotting down the stairs, his nails clicking funnily on the steps. The family Goldendoodle was a late riser, too, and proved it by plopping down on his heinie and yawning widely. He then barked once and followed Dee into the kitchen, where he proceeded to hover over his food bowl and give it a tentative sniff before digging in.

Meanwhile Dee's husband of twenty years, Tom Kelly, was juggling a skillet and a glass bowl of pancake batter, creating the perfect morning treat. A pot of coffee stood spreading its wonderful aroma through the kitchen and the table was already set for six. Dee's mom Caroline was presiding over the breakfast nook, preparing the kids' lunches.

"Mom," said Dee as she hoisted Jacob into his seat, "I told you. Maya doesn't need you to pack her a school lunch. She grabs whatever from the cafeteria." Or the Starbucks around the corner.

"I don't mind," said Mom as she added an apple to the lunch box. "Besides, the stuff they offer at schools these days is not healthy. Just a steaming pile of junk food. Unfit for man or beast."

"They have a healthy alternative," she said as she outfitted her youngest with a bib.

"You know kids. When they have a choice between a greasy burger or a plate of veggies they'll take the burger every time. Honestly, Dee, how hard is it to prepare a healthy and nutritious lunch?"

"Not hard at all. Problem is she won't eat it. I can tell you that right now. She'll dump it in the trash first chance she gets."

"No, she won't. Not when her grammy put that extra-special ingredient in there. Love," she explained.

"Love or no love—she'll trash it. Just you wait and see."

Dee's mom stubbornly pursed her lips. "No, she won't. My angel wouldn't do that to a lunch her own grammy packed. Nuh-uh."

Dee wanted to explain that Maya had stopped being an angel a long time ago but decided this was a battle she was never going to win.

"Honey," said her husband, setting down a plate of pancakes. "Can you try one? I have a feeling I forgot to add something but I don't know what it is."

Dee forked a pancake and took a bite. She grimaced. "You forgot the sugar, hon."

"Dang it," Tom murmured. "Knew I'd left something out."

Dee shared a smile with her mother. Tom really was the absent-minded professor incarnate. Not only was he a real-life professor—in economics, not chemistry—but he was as scatterbrained as they came.

"Don't you worry about a thing, Tom," said Mom. "We'll just add more jam." And to show them she meant business, she spooned a generous helping of strawberry jam onto her pancake and transferred it into her mouth. Talk about your healthy alternative.

"Kids!" Tom bellowed at the foot of the stairs. "If you don't get down here right now we're all gonna be late for school!" He darted a quick look at his wife. "And the gallery!"

"I don't know why you keep going to that place," said Mom as she added a granola bar to Scott's lunchbox. "You hired that nice girl—what's-her-name—I wanna say Trixie?"

"Holly," Dee corrected her mother, then tucked a small piece of apple into Jacob's mouth. He happily munched down on it, half the apple soon dribbling down his chin. "And the reason I keep going is because it's my gallery, Mom. I'm the one in charge."

"Sounds to me like this Trixie person is on top of things."

"Holly. And she is on top of things. But I still have to be there to handle stuff like acquisitions, communicating with the artists and collectors, setting up exhibitions…"

Mom was waving her hand. "Trixie can handle all of that stuff." She gestured to Jacob. "What she can't do is take care of your baby. That is something only you can do. Raising your kid. A few short years from now all three of your babies will be gone and that gallery will still be there waiting for you to run it. Not that I mind babysitting my grandchild," she quickly added when Dee opened her mouth to respond. "In fact I love it. But a mother leaving her child at home all day?" She shrugged. "It's just not right."

"Do you think I want to be in Seattle when I could be here at home with Jacob?"

"Oh, I know, sweetie," said her mother, reaching over to pinch her cheek as if she was the toddler, not Jacob. "But actions speak louder than words, so get your priorities straight, all right? And I'm sure Tom will back me up on this —won't you, Tom?"

Tom looked up from his study of the bowl of leftover pancake batter, a confused look on his face. At forty-eight, he actually managed to look younger than his wife, who was almost a decade his junior. How he did this, Dee did not know. "Mh?" said Tom.

"Do you or don't you agree that your wife should be home with her child instead of gallivanting around with a bunch of wannabe artists?" said Mom, enunciating clearly and distinctly as if addressing a three-year-old.

Tom's eyes shifted to Dee. "Um…"

"Oh, for crying out loud," Mom said, throwing up her hands.

"You know, if you want to stay home I'm sure we can arrange something," said Tom. "I mean financially we can definitely manage, so…"

"Look, I love my job, all right? I worked hard to set up that gallery and I can't afford to abandon it when it's still finding its feet. People who visit the Dee Kelly Gallery expect to find Dee Kelly there to greet them, not a salaried second-in-command. Besides, I'm just working mornings right now."

"You're absolutely right," said Tom soothingly, then moved over to peck a quick kiss to her brow.

"Looks like we've been vetoed, little man," said Mom, tucking a piece of pancake into Jacob's mouth.

The toddler happily gobbled up the treat, then cackled loudly. "Want more!" he yelled.

"Looks like we're getting new neighbors," said Scott, slouching into the kitchen, then draping his limp frame across a chair as if he were a bag of bones instead of a real boy.

"New neighbors?" asked Tom. "What do you mean?"

"I mean there's a moving truck backing up the driveway as we speak."

All eyes moved to the window, which offered a great view of the house next door. Scott was right. A truck was backing up the neighboring driveway, two burly movers instructing the driver with word and gesture.

"Huh," said Tom. "I didn't even know the house had been sold."

Maya waltzed into the kitchen, her eyes glued to her smartphone. "You guys, did you know that Gwen Stefani is having another baby? Isn't she, like, a thousand years old or something?"

Tom looked offended. "Gwen Stefani is my age," he said.

"Yeah, well, newsflash, Dad," said Maya. "You're old, too."

"We're getting new neighbors," Scott announced. "I hope they have a dog."

Maya's eyes snapped to the window. "Neighbors?" When she noticed the moving van, her jaw fell. "Are you kidding me right now?" She turned to her mother. "Mom—I told you we should have gotten those curtains up. Now what am I going to do?"

Scott grinned. "Relax, fuzz-face. Nobody's gonna look through your window."

"Shut up. Mom! I need curtains ASAP!"

"A girl needs her privacy," Dee's mom agreed.

"Dad!" Maya cried plaintively. "I can't have a bunch of hormonal teenagers spying on me!"

"You won't, darling," said Tom. "I'll get you those curtains. And you, Scott."

"I don't need no curtains," said Scott, shoving his fifth pancake into his mouth, this one drowning in syrup. "Unlike my sister, I got nothing to hide." Even with his mouth full of pancake, he managed a smirk, earning him a vicious scowl from Maya.

Dee's eyes happened to wander over to the clock on the kitchen wall. When she saw what time it was, she jolted into action. "You guys, we have to get moving. Scott—thank your grandmother for preparing your lunch—you, too, Maya. Chop, chop! Let's go, Kellys!"

Within five minutes, they were all racing for the exit, Dee after giving Baby Jacob a smacking kiss on the sticky cheek and promising her mother she'd be home in a couple of hours. And then they were off, leaving the kitchen a mess and Caroline shaking her head at the hullabaloo a family of five could create.

Dee then stuck her head back in. "Love you, Mom," she said. "Wouldn't know what to do without you."

"Get out of here, you," said Caroline. Then, when Dee directed a dazzling smile at her, added grudgingly, "I love you, too. Now better get going, or Trixie will be pissed."

Chapter Two

Scott took his bike from the garage and waved to Mike, who was staring at the moving van.

"Hey, buddy," said Scott as he rode up to his friend.

"You're getting new neighbors," Mike said, showing his keen powers of observation.

"Yeah. I hope they've got a dog."

"A dog? A girl, you mean."

"Girl? What girl?"

"A girl our age! A girl you can fall in love with—moon over while you're staring out of your window while she's staring out of hers." He'd pressed his hands to his chest and was looking up at the sky. "A girl so pretty you'll write her *poems* and sing her songs of *love*."

Scott eyed his friend with an expression of abject horror on his freckled face. "Are you crazy? Who needs girls?!"

"We do," said Mike as he craned his neck to catch a glimpse of whoever was moving in next door.

It shouldn't have surprised Scott that his friend felt this way. Mike was something of a dork. With his braces and his glasses he looked like one, too. Not that it bothered Scott. Mike had been his buddy ever since the Kellys moved from Medina to Issaquah where they now lived. Changing neighborhoods had been tough, but not as tough as changing schools. Making new friends had been an iffy proposition at first, and it was only when he and Mike had bonded over their shared ability to squirt orange juice out of their noses that things had started looking up again. Now they were inseparable.

"I like girls," Mike said reverently. "I like Maggie Cooper."

"Who's Maggie Cooper?"

"She's only the prettiest girl in school. Hair like spun gold. Eyes like Alaskan lakes. A nose like…" He frowned, his poetic prowess momentarily deserting him. "A nose like, um…"

"Yeah, yeah. I get the picture," said Scott, who, unlike Mike, didn't worship at the feet of girls—even if their hair was like spun gold—whatever spun gold was. "Let's get going, buddy. We're gonna be late."

As they rode off on their bikes, the two friends briefly looked back, Mike to see if his friend had just acquired a girl-next-door who could melt his barnacled heart, and Scott to try and catch a glimpse of the dog he hoped these mysterious new neighbors had brought.

❧

Maya's boyfriend was already sitting in his Ford Mustang, parked at the curb, the motor rumbling impressively. The car was a junker Mark's dad had gotten him for his sixteenth birthday but it still worked fine enough. Mark had painted it bright orange with pink stripes in deference to Maya, knowing they were her favorite colors. Maya owned her own car, a pink Mini Cooper, but Mark refused to be seen dead in the thing. Apart from that minor character flaw, the stocky Mark Dean, self-proclaimed football jock, was a surprisingly kind-hearted soul. And as the son of a lumber mill tycoon, he was also comfortably well-off. Not that that mattered a great deal to Maya, whose dad wasn't exactly a pauper either.

"You've got new neighbors," said Mark as Maya slid into the seat.

"Yeah—I hope they're nice. Not like the ones we had in Medina."

The house where they'd lived had been partially blown up

in a home invasion gone wrong. Luckily the Kelly clan had escaped the ordeal unscathed, but they'd still opted to sell the house and relocate to a part of town that wouldn't be a constant reminder of that fateful night.

"Those home invaders weren't neighbors, though, right?"

"Not technically," she admitted. The leader of the gang had been a Seattle mobster. Not a neighbor, per se, but close enough. "Let's not talk about that, Mark."

He gave her a rueful look. "I'm sorry. I won't mention it again."

Strictly speaking, she'd been the one to dredge up the wretched past, but watching Mark's expression of contrition was too much fun. She placed a hand on his cheek. "That's all right, Mark. You can always make it up to me."

His face lit up with a goofy grin. "That's more like it. Anything you want, babe."

She grimaced. "First off, don't call me babe. I hate it. Second, you can start by driving me to school. We're going to be late."

"What happened to your car?"

"Being serviced. Engine trouble." In actual fact she'd scratched the paint by hitting the mailbox last night, but she wasn't going to give Mark a reason to mock her driving skills.

Dad had bought her the car because school was now a respectable distance from her house, owing to the fact that she'd opted to stay in the same school as before, when they were still living in Medina. Seeing as she only had one more year of high school to go, it would have been a shame to switch schools like her little brother had done. One more year and she was off to college—the same university where her dad taught: the University of Washington, also known as U-Dub.

"So have you thought about filling out that college application?" she asked Mark as he eased the car away from the curb.

"Um…"

She rolled her eyes. "Mark! You promised!"

"The thing is… my dad keeps talking retirement. I don't want to let the old man down."

"Your dad has been talking retirement since he took over from his dad." She tucked a lock of blond hair behind her ear. "You know you'll be able to take that company and launch it into the stratosphere if you get an economics degree, right? My dad explained all that to you."

"I know, babe. It's just that… my grades just aren't that great."

She knew what he meant. Mark was a sweetheart, and a great athlete. What he wasn't was academically gifted. "I'm sure with a little help from me and my dad you'll do just fine. Remember, you don't have to graduate at the top of your class, Mark. You just have to graduate, period."

He emitted a noncommittal sound, then focused on the road. She gritted her teeth in disappointment. He was going to take his dad's advice and take over the lumber mill, wasn't he? Who needs a college education when you've got a perfectly good job waiting for you? And his dad had been talking retirement mainly because the Seattle weather was wreaking havoc on his arthritic joints and he was dreaming of becoming a snowbird.

What she didn't want to admit was the real reason she wanted Mark to join her at UW: the fact that she feared drifting apart if he were to join his family company while she became a college student. She punched his shoulder.

"Ow! What did you do that for?" he said.

She punched his shoulder again, harder this time.

"Hey! That's my good arm. I need that arm."

She gave him another few light punches.

"You punch like a girl," he chuckled.

"That's probably because I am a girl."

He gave her a quick sideways glance. "Are you all right?"

She did the eye roll thing again. "What do you think?"

He narrowed his eyes. "Is it that time of the month again?"

She raised her fist to give him her biggest punch yet but by now he was laughing so hard she decided not to bother. "You know what, Mark? If you don't want to go to college with me just say so. Don't give me this lame excuse of your dad says this and your dad says that."

"But my dad really says all those things!"

"Ugh," she said, and settled down in her seat, her arms folded across her chest.

"I want to go to college with you, babe," he said finally. "It's just that… I don't think I'm smart enough, okay?"

She looked up, surprised. "What are you talking about?"

"Your dad—he's like, a genius, okay? But every time he talks shop, my eyes glaze over. I don't understand a word he's saying! So I figure four years of that is going to kill me—if I ever make it that far in the first place. I'm not college material, babe—I'm just not!"

She was touched by the vulnerability he displayed. It was a side of him he rarely showed. "I'm sure that with a little tutoring from my dad—"

"But that's just it. I listen to the guy and I blank out. Completely! It's like listening to Coach Martin when he's trying to introduce a new running play. I'm not smart that way. I need to see something with my own eyes—go through the motions a couple times before I get it. And this economics gobbledygook is just… gobbledygook!"

She grinned. She got it now, and patted him on the shoulder. "Don't you worry about a thing. Just follow my lead and you'll make it through four years of gobbledygook just fine."

Now that she knew what ailed him, she knew exactly what to do about it, too.

He gave her a curious glance. "Uh-oh," he said. "I know that look."

"What look?"

"You've got some kind of plan, don't you?"

"Of course I've got a plan. Never go through life without a plan. Isn't that what I keep telling you?"

He gave her a lost-puppy look. "Uh-huh," he said tentatively.

She patted his shoulder again. "I've got this," she assured him.

"That's what I'm afraid of," he murmured.

Chapter Three

As Tom drove the family Toyota Sienna out of the driveway he stared so hard at the moving van he almost clipped the mailbox.

"Watch out!" Dee cried.

He stomped on the brake and the car screeched to a standstill. "I wonder who they are," he said as he eased the car into reverse and backed up. "First thing tonight let's go over and introduce ourselves." Already he was painting a mental picture of their new neighbor. A professor, just like himself—possibly in a less technical field. Archeology? Or something really cool like robotics or artificial intelligence? They could chat over the hedge—exchange ideas while their wives socialized over preprandial martinis on the patio. Or he could show his new neighbor his newly acquired collection of model trains and tracks.

In his mind's eye he was already picturing himself and this kindly man who was a few years his senior rolling up their collective sleeves and constructing a train track in their combined backyards, just like Walt Disney did back in the day. Wouldn't that be something?

"Do you want me to drive, honey?" asked his wife, giving him a worried look.

"Mh? Oh, no, I'm fine. Just wondering... Do people still bring over a freshly baked pie? Or is that too old-fashioned?"

"We can bring a pie," said Dee. "Or a bottle of wine. Just not sure if they're..."

"The pie-eating or the wine-drinking kind of people," Tom finished the sentence. "Gotcha. Probably we should—"

"—spy out who they are before we commit ourselves to one or the other."

Now they were both staring, as Tom drove the car at a snail's pace past the neighboring house.

"I don't see anyone," said Tom. "Maybe they sent the movers ahead of them."

"Or maybe it's Brad Pitt and he'll move in under the cloak of darkness and we'll never get to see him as he'll be coming and going through a secret passageway in the basement."

Tom gave his wife a curious look. "Brad Pitt? Really?"

"I wouldn't mind if Angelina Jolie moved in so you can't mind if Brad Pitt moves in."

"You do know that Brangelina is no more, right?"

"Of course I know. Brad is single now," she said with a touch of wistfulness.

They stared some more. "I just hope they're nice people," said Tom. With a keen interest in model trains who didn't mind getting their hands dirty while laying track.

"And I hope they have a boy Scott's age and a girl Maya's age and the kids can bond."

"Don't forget a dog who's Ralph's age and a baby Jacob's age."

He touched his foot down on the accelerator and soon they were cruising through the neighborhood, which consisted entirely of similar houses to their own. After last year's home invasion, the Kelly family mantra was not to stand out, and stand out they definitely did not. They drove a nice sensible family car, occupied a nice sensible single-family home, and lived a nice sensible family life. Nothing to see here, folks. Move right along!

§▲

After he'd dropped off his wife at the art gallery, Tom proceeded towards his own place of business, the university he called his home away from home. Breezing into his office, he plunked down his floppy brown leather satchel, drew a hand through his floppy brown hair and dropped down in his swivel chair, booting up his computer as he did. Before he had a chance to check his schedule, a knock on the door alerted him of his first visitor.

"Come in!" he boomed.

The door opened and a head poked in. The head was pale and festooned with red spots, the few remaining hairs on the top awkwardly combed to cover the acreage.

"Hey, Tom," said Elliott Lusky, head of the history department.

"Elliott," said Tom jovially. "So have you thought about my offer?"

Elliott shook his bulbous head mournfully. "No can do, I'm afraid. The wife has been nagging me to take her on one of those Alaskan cruises and she's earmarked every last penny in our savings account for that particular purpose. Terribly inconvenient, I know."

Tom leaned back in his chair. "Can't you tell her you're allergic to Alaska or something?" Ever since Tom had seen a documentary about Walt Disney's love for model trains he'd been dreaming of building his own, smaller version of the impressive set Uncle Walt had built in his backyard in the fifties. To this end he needed allies—friends he could share his new passion with. And Elliott was just such a friend. Unfortunately the tubby little man was displaying an awful lot of sales resistance.

"I'm afraid not," said Elliott with a look of apology on his face. "She wanted to go last year. I managed to stave off the disaster by claiming Alaska was in fact part of Canada and we'd need a visa, which we'd never get as I've been declared persona non grata in Canuck country ever since I got drunk and disorderly on a high school trip to Montreal."

"You don't need a visa to visit Canada."

"I know that. The point is that Esther doesn't—or didn't." He frowned. "Curse the internet. Not only does she know I lied to her about Alaska being a part of Canada, she's starting to suspect I made up that whole thing about being arrested in Montreal."

"Were you ever arrested in Montreal?"

Tom's colleague rearranged his features into an appropriate expression of contrition. "No, I was not. An exceedingly nice police officer once cautioned me for jaywalking, though."

"I don't think that counts."

"I don't think so either. Anyway, as it stands she's already booked the tickets so it looks like I'm in for it. I'll have to traipse along while she watches humpback whales cavort in the surf or glides down one of those wretched glaciers."

"Do people actually glide down glaciers? I would have thought that was dangerous. People have been known to tumble down a crevasse never to be seen again."

A gleam of hope lit up the distinguished history professor's face. But then he shook his head, the gleam extinguished. "With my luck that will never happen." He checked his watch. "Have to run, Tom. I've got a class to teach on the

Borgia family." He stared before him for a moment. "They were very fond of arsenic, those Borgias. Liked to poison their husbands. And their wives. Excruciatingly painful, death by arsenic. Very effective."

And with these words he held up his hand and withdrew, gently closing the door.

ABOUT NIC

Nic Saint is the pen name for writing couple Nick and Nicole Saint. They've penned novels in the romance, cat sleuth, middle grade, suspense, comedy and cozy mystery genres. Nicole has a background in accounting and Nick in political science and before being struck by the writing bug the Saints worked odd jobs around the world (including massage therapist in Mexico, gardener in Italy, restaurant manager in India, and Berlitz teacher in Belgium).

When they're not writing they enjoy Christmas-themed Hallmark movies (whether it's Christmas or not), all manner of pastry, comic books, a daily dose of yoga (to limber up those limbs), and spoiling their big red tomcat Tommy.

www.nicsaint.com

The Mysteries of Max

Purrfect Murder

Purrfectly Deadly

Purrfect Revenge

Box Set 1 (Books 1-3)

Purrfect Heat

Purrfect Crime

Purrfect Rivalry

Box Set 2 (Books 4-6)

Purrfect Peril

Purrfect Secret

Purrfect Alibi

Box Set 3 (Books 7-9)

Purrfect Obsession

Purrfect Betrayal

Purrfectly Clueless

Box Set 4 (Books 10-12)

Purrfectly Royal

Purrfect Cut

Purrfect Trap

Purrfectly Hidden

Purrfect Kill

Purrfect Santa

Purrfectly Flealess

Nora Steel

Murder Retreat

The Kellys

Murder Motel

Death in Suburbia

Emily Stone

Murder at the Art Class

Washington & Jefferson

First Shot

Alice Whitehouse

Spooky Times

Spooky Trills

Spooky End

Spooky Spells

Ghosts of London

Between a Ghost and a Spooky Place

Public Ghost Number One

Ghost Save the Queen

Box Set 1 (Books 1-3)

A Tale of Two Harrys

Ghost of Girlband Past

Ghostlier Things

Charleneland

Deadly Ride

Final Ride

Neighborhood Witch Committee

Witchy Start

Witchy Worries

Witchy Wishes

Saffron Diffley

Crime and Retribution

Vice and Verdict

Felonies and Penalties (Saffron Diffley Short 1)

The B-Team

Once Upon a Spy

Tate-à-Tate

Enemy of the Tates

Ghosts vs. Spies

The Ghost Who Came in from the Cold

Witchy Fingers

Witchy Trouble

Witchy Hexations

Witchy Possessions

Witchy Riches

Box Set 1 (Books 1-4)

The Mysteries of Bell & Whitehouse

One Spoonful of Trouble

Two Scoops of Murder

Three Shots of Disaster

Box Set 1 (Books 1-3)

A Twist of Wraith

A Touch of Ghost

A Clash of Spooks

Box Set 2 (Books 4-6)

The Stuffing of Nightmares

A Breath of Dead Air

An Act of Hodd

Box Set 3 (Books 7-9)

A Game of Dons

Standalone Novels

When in Bruges

The Whiskered Spy

ThrillFix

Homejacking

The Eighth Billionaire

The Wrong Woman

Made in the USA
Coppell, TX
05 August 2020

32447365R00134